THE MAN I THOUGHT I LOVED

TWO-FACED #2

E. L. TODD

HARTWICK PUBLISHING

Hartwick Publishing

The Man I Thought I Loved

Copyright © 2020 by E. L. Todd

All rights reserved.

No part of this book may be reproduced in any form or by any electronic or mechanical means, including information storage and retrieval systems, without written permission from the author, except for the use of brief quotations in a book review.

CONTENTS

1. Dax	1
2. Carson	11
3. Dax	21
4. Carson	31
5. Dax	51
6. Carson	77
7. Dax	109
8. Carson	125
9. Dax	133
10. Carson	145
11. Dax	149
12. Carson	155
13. Carson	171
14. Dax	181
15. Dax	193
16. Carson	205
17. Dax	221
18. Carson	243
19. Carson	259
20. Carson	275
You Might Also Like...	283

ONE

DAX

She disappeared from my life.

I couldn't text her because she blocked me.

When I texted Charlie, I got no response either.

They didn't show up to the basketball game on Wednesday.

I didn't show up at her door again because it seemed pointless.

So, I let her go...even though it hurt like hell.

I sat in my office and stared out the window, constantly distracted by the final conversation I'd had with Carson. Her intelligence made her difficult to argue with, and she wove a painful narrative that made even me hate myself.

I'd thought it was a harmless lie, but now I realized how terrible it truly was.

I'd do anything to take it back.

Renee walked inside. "Are you sure you're alright? Every time I see you, you look worse and worse."

"Yeah." I hadn't told her what happened because it was too painful to share.

She took a seat and gave me an incredulous look. "Dax, come on. Did something happen with Carson?"

I couldn't hide it any longer. "Carson knows the truth."

"She knows?" She tilted her head slightly. "That sounds like you didn't tell her?"

I shook my head. "Her colleague was supposed to interview me for that editorial piece...but they sent her instead."

"Oh geez."

"Yeah..."

"What now?"

"I tried to talk to her, but she wanted nothing to do with me. That was a week ago."

She crossed her legs and ignored the folder she'd brought to my office to discuss. "I'm sorry, Dax."

"Don't be. It's all my fault." I should have told her sooner.

"And that's it?"

"Yeah. She doesn't want to see me anymore."

She looked out the window. "If you really like her, you should do something."

"No. She made her stance perfectly clear."

"But you're a good man, Dax. You're worth giving a second chance."

"You don't know Carson," I said with a painful chuckle.

She was quiet for a long time, as if the conversation was over. "What happened to the article?"

"Kinda just got dropped."

"Well, I have an idea."

"Hmm?"

"Ask to do it—and specifically request her."

I stared at my sister for a while, finding the suggestion ridiculous. "Force her to spend time with someone she hates?"

"She doesn't hate you."

"I don't know about that..."

"And work on the best friend. Convince him, and you can convince her."

"He's loyal."

"But I doubt he thinks you're a bad guy because you're not, Dax. Sure, you could have handled it better, but you deserve another chance. Fight for her. She sounds special—and you can't just let her go. If she doesn't give you a second chance, you make her give you a second chance. Because you're a very incredible man. She could have an incredible man if she's forced to see it."

SINCE MATT and Jeremy were still seeing each other, it was easy for me to figure out a time when I could run into

Charlie. The three of them went out for a drink after work, and Jeremy passed the information on to me.

They were sitting at the bar, watching a game on the TV when I walked in.

Jeremy saw me first. "Hey, man." I clapped him on the shoulder before I did the same to Matt.

Charlie glanced over his shoulder to look at me, but he gave no reaction. Stoic and cold, he turned back to the TV and drank from his beer.

Charlie was the more reasonable one, the calm that canceled out Carson's fire. Maybe she would never understand why I'd lied, but he might. It was worth the shot. Instead of taking the empty seat beside Jeremy, I took the one beside Charlie.

He looked straight ahead, his elbows on the bar, his eyes on the TV.

"I'll take a scotch," I said to the waitress.

She gave me a smile to earn a big tip before she poured the scotch in front of me. "There you are." She moved away to take care of the other guys who'd come in to watch the game.

I took a drink.

Charlie pretended I didn't exist.

"How's it going, man?"

He grabbed his beer and took a drink.

"The silent treatment... Cliché."

He turned to me, provoked by the statement. "What do you want, Dax?"

"To know how it's going. Exactly what I asked."

He faced forward again. "Look, we can't be friends like we used to. I'm sure you've figured that out."

This was not going well. I took another drink of my scotch. "That's too bad."

He watched the game like nothing happened.

Charlie didn't have the rage Carson did. He was her best friend, but he wasn't an overprotective brother figure threatening to kick my ass outside the bar. He simply wasn't an aggressive person. That was probably why he was a journalist—because he didn't get emotional. "I've had a really shitty week."

He didn't turn my way, but his body tightened noticeably.

"I really fucked up with Carson. And I wish I could take it back."

He looked down into his beer. "Why are you telling me this?"

"Because you're the brain, and she's the heart."

He turned back to me, his eyes curious at my words.

"You know, you're more logical and pragmatic. She's emotional, passionate, spontaneous. Those aren't bad attributes. I mean, it's what attracted me to her in the first place. But right now, it's working against me."

"If you think you're going to get her back...it's not going to happen."

It felt like he'd pressed his shoe right against my chest and cracked it. "I'd still like us to be friends."

He stared into my eyes, his dirty-blond hair combed back.

"Charlie, I never meant to hurt her. I know I should have told her the truth, but honestly, I haven't met a woman I've actually cared about since my ex-wife. I wasn't expecting to feel that way for a long time, so stumbling across Carson was unexpected."

"If you'd told her sooner, if she'd heard it from you, none of this would have happened."

"I know. I shouldn't have dragged my feet."

"You should have told her the moment you knew she wouldn't care less about your money."

I nodded. "Yeah, I should have. But we were already in pretty deep at that point."

"Or when you asked her to be exclusive, you should have told her then."

I sighed. "Charlie, we can play this game all night long. We can look back and point out every mistake and what I should have done better. But at the end of the day, I was just trying to find something real, and that's impossible when women know I'm a billionaire. I never know if they want me for me or my wallet—and it's usually my wallet."

He nodded slightly, like he understood. "Dax, I totally get it. I don't think you're a bad guy."

No one understood that kind of wealth until they had it. From their point of view, being rich was only a good thing, would only bring about positive outcomes. But they had no idea how much it changed the perception of everyone around them. They said it was lonely at the top, which was true. Sometimes people were so envious that they hated you. Sometimes they were so greedy that they obsessed over you. Sometimes they were insecure and wanted nothing to do with you. Sometimes people kissed your ass, when they normally wouldn't give you the time of day. No single relationship was real...except what I had with my sister and a few friends. "I wasn't sneaking around behind her back. I wasn't married. The lie was harmless...for the most part."

"Yeah, I get it. For anyone else, it wouldn't be a problem. But after everything Carson has been through, it's just too much. Her ex really fucked her up. It wasn't just what he did, but the fact that he lied to her face every day and she believed him. She was humiliated."

"I know that feeling just as well as she does."

"But you had your shield up and asked her to take hers down."

I sighed in disappointment.

"I'm sorry, man. I understand your point of view. But I also understand hers. It just wasn't meant to be."

"I still want her, Charlie."

He dropped his gaze.

"I finally found a good woman, and I don't want to let her go. I want another chance."

He shook his head. "Not gonna happen."

"Maybe it could happen if you talked to her."

He cringed then rubbed the back of his neck. "Man, you did not just go there."

"Come on, Charlie. You know I'm a good guy. Yes, I lied about who I was, but everything else about me is totally real."

He stared down into his beer.

"Who wouldn't want their best friend to date a billionaire?"

He gave a slight chuckle. "She couldn't care less about your money, man. If anything, it's a turn-off."

Fuck, why did I mess this up? "If you can honestly tell me there's a better guy for her, that there's somebody who would treat her better than I would, I'll let this go. But there's a ton of scumbags out there, and I'm not one of them. I get along with all of you perfectly. I'm not some stuck-up suit. I'm impressed by her success rather than intimidated by it. She's a lot of woman, and she needs a lot of man. I'm definitely man enough."

He continued to stare at his beer before he lifted his gaze and looked at me.

"You know it's true, man."

He sighed deeply.

I stared at him, hoping for the answer that would give me a chance.

"I'll think about it."

That was the most I was going to get, so I chose to appreciate it. "Thanks."

He nodded and turned back to the TV.

"Regardless of the outcome, I'd like it if we could be friends. Jeremy is with Matt, and Nathan is with Kat. It's not like you're never going to see me again. Plus, you aren't the type of guy to hold a grudge."

"Yeah, I guess it's fine."

"And Carson doesn't strike me as the kind of person who would tell you to stop talking to me either."

He shook his head. "No."

"How is she, by the way?" She'd blocked my number, so I couldn't contact her. I didn't want to show up at her office or her apartment unannounced because that just seemed to piss her off. When she'd screamed at me, she didn't seem heartbroken, just furious, but she was also the type of woman that would never show weakness, that would never let me see her scars.

"She's fine." Charlie watched the TV.

I couldn't read between the words, couldn't see the truth in his vagueness. I just hoped she really was fine…but I suspected she wasn't.

TWO
CARSON

"You've got to be kidding me." I stood in front of Vince's desk, appalled by what I'd heard.

"His assistant asked for you—specifically."

That rat bastard. "He asked for Vivica last time. Send her."

"Carson, is this going to be a problem?" He had nothing but respect for me, but now he cocked his head and eyed me with an eyebrow raised, his eyes enlarged through his glasses.

I never said no. That was how I got ahead here. No one else wanted the story in Iraq, but I took it. So, saying no to an interview with a billionaire seemed odd, and I definitely wouldn't air my dirty laundry and let my personal life affect my work. But that motherfucker purposely asked for me so I would have to see him. "No."

"Then take care of it. The meeting is in a few hours."

"Got it." The second I turned around, I let my anger overcome my features. I shut the door behind me and walked past Charlie's cubicle on the way to mine.

He looked up and turned his head to follow me with his eyes, his eyebrows high in alarm.

I got to my desk and collapsed into the chair, my hands digging in my hair as I let out a quiet growl.

"Did you just get fired or something?" Charlie leaned against the desk and lowered his voice.

"No. Worse."

His eyes narrowed. "Did he put you on the *Home and Lifestyle* section?"

"Okay, not that bad." I dropped my hands into my lap. "I guess Dax has requested me specifically to do his editorial."

Charlie didn't react right away. "So he can get in a room with you."

"Yep. You know, I respected him for accepting my rejection and disappearing. But it looks like I was wrong."

He crossed his arms over his chest. "What are you going to do?"

"My job."

"It's been a week since he was at the apartment. Have you cooled down at all?"

I didn't allow myself to think about him, not because it made me angry, but because it hurt. "No."

He stared at me. "I know what he did was wrong, but he's not a bad guy."

"You're kidding with this, right?" I snapped.

"I'm just saying he's not an adulterer or something. He was burned really badly by his gold-digging ex-wife, and he just wanted to find someone who wanted him, not his money. He had good intentions."

"So, you think it's okay that he lied?" I snapped.

"Not at all. I'm just saying, have some perspective on this. We know bad people. We know what bad people are capable of. Dax does not fall into that category. If you don't want to get back together with him, that's fine. But maybe tone down the hostility a bit. Don't march in there throwing daggers."

I knew he was right. My anger came from the pain, which I was entitled to, but Dax wasn't evil. "Fine."

He got off the desk and straightened. "Good luck."

"Can you put on a wig and do it for me?"

He grinned before he turned away. "I think my dick would throw him off."

"Would you whip it out during the interview?" I asked with a raised eyebrow.

"No. But if he thought I was you, he might try to take off my pants."

I CHECKED in at the front desk like last time, then took a seat.

My heart wasn't racing like last time because I knew exactly what to expect. I'd walk in there and see Dax in his $10,000 suit and his $20,000 watch with his big-ass desk that he'd probably fucked an assistant on.

I was livid he'd summoned me here for this interview. It was below the belt, completely unfair. But I was a professional, and I would do my job.

"He's ready for you." The petite blonde walked to the double doors and opened one for me.

"Thanks." I stepped inside and saw him sitting on one of the couches, a tray that held a pitcher of water and two glasses on the table, along with a bottle of wine and two glasses. He leaned back and was relaxed, one ankle resting on the opposite knee. But he'd ditched the suit and wore jeans and a t-shirt, just the way he'd dressed whenever I'd seen him.

His eyes shifted to my face, his expression impassive. He studied me, as if he were waiting for me to scream at him, to let me get it all out before he said anything. One arm was on the armrest, while the other beside him. His shirt flattened against his frame, showing how tight his stomach was, how strong his chest was. Stubble was on his jaw, thicker than usual, like he'd skipped the shave for days. His brown eyes were empty and unreadable.

I approached the other couch and took a seat, holding my notebook and recorder. I was in a pencil skirt and a tight blouse with pumps. The clothing was professional, but I preferred jeans and a top. I turned on the recorder and set it on the table before I clicked my pen and held the tip to the notebook where my notes were.

His eyes never left my face.

I lifted my chin and looked at him, ignored his handsome stare, the same intense gaze he gave me the night we met, and just pushed through it. "You stepped up to the position when your father passed away. How was—"

"Are we really going to do this?" His deep voice shattered my confidence because it was so powerful. When he was in his element, he was authoritative and superior, producing all the energy in the room like he was the sun.

I kept my cool. "You asked me to come here and interview you. I'm doing my job." I held his gaze and remained aloof, even though my heart started to race. I wanted to fidget with my pen, but I forced myself to be still, to hold my ground against this man who had quickly turned the tables.

"Then ask better questions." He bent his arm and rested his fingers slightly against his jaw, absentmindedly touching the coarse hair that used to rub against the inside of my thighs when he kissed me in my most intimate place.

"If you have better questions, maybe you should just type up your answers and email them to my office. You know, save us both some time."

His expression didn't change, but his eyes developed a tint of anger. "I grew up wealthy. My grandfather founded this company, gave it to my father, and upon his death, it was given to me. Most people would say I should be grateful for what I have, and while I am, I grew up with a target on my back. A lot of eyes were on me, eyes that I couldn't see." He brushed his fingers against the coarse hair of his face, his eyes on me and hardly blinking. "One of those eyes belonged to Rose—my ex-wife. I'd been doing the playboy lifestyle for a long time, spending money I didn't earn, impressing people who didn't matter. Rose had one thing on her mind when she met me, and I was too naïve to see it, too arrogant. She used me, took half my money in the divorce, and now she owns half of my part of this company, my family's legacy—because of my stupidity."

I remained still on the couch and tried to keep my heart closed to his story. I didn't want him to break me down, to make me sympathetic so I would forgive what he did to me.

"It haunts me every day. My sister works here with me, and she resents me for it…not that I blame her. My family told me to get a prenup, but I didn't listen. It's not about the money, but the way I disregarded my family's wishes, the way I assumed I knew everything…when I knew nothing at all." He shifted his gaze for the first time, looking toward his desk and the window behind it. With those dark eyes and unbelievable good looks, he could make anyone forgive him for everything. "Safe to say, I'm pretty fucked up from it." He turned back to me. "After my divorce, I went back to the playboy, manwhore bullshit. But I couldn't do it anymore. It's the same shit just on a different night. It's the same girl but with a different face. Even though my marriage was a sham, there were aspects I liked, and having a real connection to someone is far more fulfilling than casual sex. I didn't expect to find someone I liked anytime soon…but then I met you." He focused his stare on my face, those brown eyes shining with sincerity. "It would be easy to argue that pretending to be something I'm not is despicable, staging an apartment to make it seem like I live there is disgusting. But I'm tired of my billionaire title. People say money doesn't matter, but it matters to everyone. It skews all my relationships, and I'm tired of it. I'm sorry I hurt you, but I don't regret what I did—because I found you."

I had been understanding of his story until that point. "You don't regret lying to me?"

He dropped his elbow from the armrest and gripped his calf instead. "Think about it. What would have happened if I'd told you the truth right off the bat?"

"I don't know because it didn't happen."

"Our relationship would have played out completely differently, and you know it. You either would have wanted me more because of my money or wanted me less. You can sit there and say money doesn't matter to you, but if my wealth is a turn-off to you, then it does matter. You never would have given me a real chance."

"And that would be for me to decide. I probably wouldn't have been interested since I deal with rich suits all the time and they think they're entitled to do whatever they want—which is exactly what you did." Because the badge was around my neck and I was on the clock, I could speak in a normal voice, even though we were alone. I remained professional and calm, like the interview was actually taking place.

His eyes narrowed on my face. "Not the same thing at all."

"I disagree." I didn't take a single note because none of this would go in the article anyway.

He held my gaze for a long time, comfortable in the silence, unaffected by the intensity coming from both of us as invisible balls of energy. "You were cold and distant when we met, treating me like an object instead of a person, and I was understanding when you told me about your divorce. I get it. I'd appreciate the same understanding now, in light of what I told you."

"Dax, if you'd sat me down at dinner and told me all this yourself, I would have been understanding. I'm not unreasonable. But you let it go on for so long and then let me find out in the worst way possible."

With his eyes locked on mine, he inhaled a deep breath.

"I'm sorry about Rose. I'm sorry someone used you like that. It's disgusting. Since you knew what happened to me, you would know that I would understand the pain, the humiliation. But you didn't confide in me. Instead, you continued to deceive me. When were you going to tell me?"

"When I took you to the dinner we had planned."

"You say that, but who knows? You wanted to start screwing without condoms while keeping me in the dark."

He closed his eyes for a second. "I got carried away because every single time we're together, it's fucking fire. And then you wanted to screw in the alleyway, which is already hot enough, and you wanted to ditch the protection because I didn't have any. You remember what I said? I said no. Because I knew I had to tell you first. Let's not forget that night."

He did deny me, and now I knew why. "I'm not sure what you want from me, Dax."

His body stilled at my words, and his eyes narrowed a little farther, like my statement was genuinely surprising. "You."

"That's not going to happen. I don't know you."

He leaned forward, his arms resting on his knees. "Then get to know me. Let's start over."

"I don't want to start over. I want to move on."

"Carson—"

"Listen to me." I held up my hand to silence him. "Look, I understand where you're coming from, why you did what you did. It's a reasonable thing to do, to hide your money to make sure you fall for someone who falls for you and not the wealth attached to your name. I don't think you're a bad person because of it. But I'm still so fragile." I had to pause to take a breath, to digest the pain I suddenly felt, to let the water in my eyes disappear again. "I'm still broken. When I was married, I loved my husband with everything I had, and it's not just his infidelity that hurts, but all the lies…the lies to my face. Charlie encouraged me out of my comfort zone when I knew I wasn't ready. I'm too sensitive to handle this, to bounce back like nothing happened. If I'm going to be in a relationship with someone, it has to be based on a foundation of complete honesty. No surprises. I want to forgive you and just move on, but that's not me, not in my current state. I'm sorry, but it's not going to happen…and there's nothing you can do to change that."

He bowed his head and looked at his hands, his shoulders sagging with defeat.

I wasn't sure if I should just get up and leave…or proceed with the interview. The room was filled with so many of our emotions.

He cleared his throat. "I shouldn't have rushed things with you. I should have just left them alone. I should have been patient." He raised his head and looked at me. "I was selfish because I wanted you, and I took this relationship in a direction you weren't ready for, without being honest about who I was." He shook his head. "I see that now…and I'm sorry."

Now it was hard to look at him because I could feel his pain, his regret. I was pretty astute at reading people, and I could read him so clearly. It didn't matter that his face was still blank, because I could feel the pain radiating from his soul. It filled the room, changed the energy. "We can still be friends."

He lifted his chin and looked at me, his hands together, his body still leaning forward. He stared at me for a long time, his eyes slightly shifting back and forth. "I thought you had enough friends?" He smiled slightly, forced it to stretch across his lips, but no amount of force could make it reach his eyes.

I remembered the words I'd said to him at the bar, the cold reaction I gave that resulted in him putting me in my place. He was the one hurt in that moment, but he tried to lighten the mood, because he accepted my answer. The conversation was finally over. He would stop trying. It was done. "I can make room for one more."

THREE

DAX

I was just about to leave the office when Renee walked inside.

"I'm going to head out." I placed my laptop inside my satchel then placed the strap over my shoulder. "You want a ride?"

"Your driver doesn't mind?"

"He's paid too much to mind." I walked out of the office with her by my side. We entered the elevator and hit the button to the lobby.

She kept glancing at me.

"What?" I could see her blurry reflection in the steel doors, see her turn to look at me.

"How did your interview go?"

It didn't go the way I wanted, but I'd accepted the results. "It's not going to happen."

"Really?" she asked in surprise. "She really can't forgive you?"

"No. But it's fine...I understand."

"I think she's being unreasonable—"

"Really, it's okay." The doors opened, and I let her step out first.

"How is it okay?" she asked. "I thought you really liked her."

"I do. But it's just not meant to be. She wasn't ready for a relationship in the first place, and I kinda steered her into it. I was selfish. I see that now."

"Wanting to be with someone isn't selfish, Dax."

"It is when you aren't honest about who you are." I walked through the double doors to the car waiting for me. I opened the back door for her. "I don't want to talk about this anymore, Renee. Let's just move on."

She looked at me before she lowered herself into the car, like she wanted to say something to make this better, but there was nothing she could say.

I'd made my bed. Now I had to lie in it.

She got inside.

I got into the other side.

The car took off, the driver already knowing to take Renee to her penthouse.

I looked out the window, my arm on the armrest.

"You seem okay with it."

"She said we can be friends."

"Then it sounds like the conversation ended well."

"Yeah, I'd say so."

She watched me from her seat, having that same sad look in her eyes the way Mom used to. "You'll find the right person, Dax. She's out there...and she's amazing."

I didn't want to go back to my old lifestyle, but I didn't want to date either. Both seemed like a lot of work for very little reward. The positive relationships in my life gave me more happiness than the cash in my bank account, so I would just focus on that. In time, the right person would come along, when I was ready and she was ready, so there was no rush. It would happen when it was supposed to happen. "So, still seeing your mystery man, William?"

"Yes." Her mood improved, a slight smile coming into her features. "He seems like the real deal."

"You won't know until I check him out."

She rolled her eyes. "You'll just scare him off."

"No, but I'll try. If he sticks around, then he's solid."

"How about you just be pleasant company instead?"

I turned to her. "Does this mean this dinner is happening?"

"Maybe..."

"Good. Let me know when and where."

"He's actually the one who's interested in this dinner. I'd avoid it forever if I could."

"Really?" With my elbow on the armrest, I turned my head toward her, my interest piqued. "He's the one who wants to meet me?"

"I couldn't believe it either. I warned him about your obnoxiousness, but he still wants to do it."

"Sounds like he's serious if he's willing to go to toe-to-toe with me."

She rolled her eyes. "Why does this have to be a hostile meeting?"

I chuckled. "Renee, I'm kidding. Everything will be fine… unless I don't like him."

"You will like him. And honestly, I don't care if you don't like him."

I grinned. "Yes, you do."

She looked out the window and shook her head.

"Come on, admit it."

"I don't," she repeated.

"Whatever you say, sis."

She kept her eyes out the window, playing with her earring. We spent the rest of the drive in silence until we pulled up to her building. She opened the door but turned to me before she got out. "Alright, I do care."

"Knew it."

"So, it would mean the world to me if you would try as hard as he's going to try."

I watched her leave the car and shut the door behind her. "Always."

NATHAN and I met up after a day at the office. We got a couple beers and sat in the booth, waiting for Jeremy to join us whenever he got his ass over here.

"How are things with Kat?"

He drank from his beer and looked at the TV behind me. "She's pretty cool. She's laid-back, easy to talk to, got great style...I like her."

"See it going anywhere?"

He shrugged. "You know me, I like to take things slow."

"You mean, never commit until you're coerced," I teased.

"Yeah, same thing. What about you? That whole thing with Carson is really done?"

I nodded. "Yep."

He shook his head. "What kind of chick gets pissed when she finds out her man is a secret billionaire? No offense, man, but I think you dodged a bullet."

The contrary, actually. The fact that she didn't want me even though she knew my status made it harder to let her go. She was the real deal, and I'd screwed it up so badly, beyond repair. When she'd told me how she felt, it gave me the closure to move on, because it really was never going to work. Friendship was all we would ever have. "Didn't dodge a bullet. I like that she doesn't care about my money."

He shrugged. "The fact that she won't look past it makes her seem dramatic."

She was just my friend now and I didn't have to defend her, but I felt obligated. "She's not dramatic. I understand her perspective, and it's fine." I wouldn't share the intimate details about her marriage and her heartbreak. It was no one's business.

"I guess I'll always dislike her for hurting you."

"Well, don't. Because I'm fine with it."

He watched me for a while, pity in his eyes. "She's the first woman you felt anything for since Rose. And now you're just fine being friends?"

I shrugged. "I'm not going to fight for a woman who doesn't want me. She made her decision, and I respect it. No drama. No hard feelings. Let's just move on."

He shifted his gaze back to the TV. "Alright, if you say so."

Jeremy walked in a moment later and joined us. "Hey, what are you bitches talking about?"

"Carson," Nathan said.

"Oh yeah, so that's really over?" Jeremy asked me.

I didn't want to have this conversation again. "We decided to just be friends."

"Is that going to be a problem for us?" Jeremy asked. "Because Matt and I are joined at the hip." Jeremy was lean and athletic, working for a fashion designer as a photographer. He was artistic and creative, and his blond hair and blue eyes made him look like a model who should be on the other side of his camera. "What about you and Kat?"

"We're still seeing each other." Nathan had always been reserved, never being vulnerable or putting his feelings on the line. He had his heart broken a long time ago and never learned how to drop his guard. He had dark hair and green eyes, with a muscular build despite the fact that he sat in a chair all day at the office.

Jeremy turned back to me. "So, is that going to be weird?"

"Not at all," I answered, holding my beer. "We can be friends."

"You're sure?" Jeremy asked.

"Yes," I repeated.

"Come on, look at him," Nathan said. "This guy can get pussy every night of the week. He's fine. He'll be over her in a couple days."

"True," Jeremy said. "You'll bounce back."

"Definitely." I drank from my beer and didn't correct them because letting the assumption linger was the best way for this conversation to end. "I'm going to get another beer." I scooted out of the booth and walked to the bar, setting my bottle on the counter and ordering another.

"I feel like every time I see you, you're drinking."

I turned to see Charlie beside me. "When you don't see me, I'm drinking more." I smiled and extended my hand to shake his. "What are you doing here?"

"I'm meeting someone." He was a lot more relaxed around me compared to our last interaction, so Carson must have said positive things about our conversation.

"Like, a lady?"

He nodded.

"Who is she?"

"I was in Brooklyn, working on an assignment, and we bumped into each other at a coffee shop."

"Cool." I took the beer from the waitress and twisted off the cap before I took a drink. "So, still no Denise, then?"

He shrugged. "I can't be celibate, right? Guy's gotta eat."

I chuckled. "True." I was fine not seeing anybody for the time being because it hadn't even been two weeks since I'd tied Carson to her headboard and fucked her good. But give it another week, and I'd probably start to get anxious.

"So…Carson told me about the other day."

"Yeah, we decided to be friends."

He studied me, as if he expected a rebuttal. "You're okay with that?"

"Yeah."

He raised an eyebrow.

"Wasn't meant to be."

"So, you don't want me to try to change her mind?"

I shook my head. "No. But thanks."

"Alright. But for the record, I did want this to work. I really pushed her on you because I thought you would be great together."

"I appreciate that, man. But she and I never had a chance."

"Are you going to keep dating the way you did before?"

I shrugged. "No idea. I'm not really interested in dating right now. Carson was an anomaly. Wasn't expecting to find her. She's a needle in a haystack, but I found her too quickly. I'll probably just fuck around for a while."

"Guy's gotta eat, right?" He clinked his beer against mine.

I nodded.

"Well, enjoy your date."

"Thanks."

I turned away.

"Hey, you think it'd be weird if we came back for basketball?"

I faced him again. "I don't have a problem with that."

"Cool. We'll see you then." He raised his glass to me before I walked away.

I did the same to him before I returned to my friends.

FOUR

CARSON

"He seemed totally fine with it." Charlie twisted off the cap to his beer and drank it.

"That's good." I was at the dining table with my laptop open, working on all my projects at once.

"Are you okay with that?" He eyed me from the kitchen, his eyebrow raised.

"Yeah. Why wouldn't I be?"

He studied me before he turned to the fridge and peeked inside, looking for something to make for dinner. "I'm going to play basketball with him on Wednesday. You want to join?"

I said we would stay friends, and while it would be weird for a while, it would get better. My friends were dating his friends, so I'd probably see him pretty often. And I was still writing that editorial piece and I never actually interviewed him, so I'd have to go back. "Sure. It gets me to exercise."

"Which you need since you eat like a horse." He pulled out a couple things and set them on the counter.

I stuck out my tongue at him. "What's for dinner?"

"Just proved my point."

"Oh, shut up." I grabbed my beer and took a drink.

"I was thinking shrimp tacos, since the shrimp is gonna go bad tomorrow."

"Good idea."

A knock sounded on the door.

"I'm not expecting anyone," he said. "You?"

"Nope." I walked to the front door and saw my sister on the other side. "Hey, girl. What's up?"

"Thought I'd swing by and see what you're up to." Her hair was curled, and she was in a sundress with heels.

"You look way too hot to just randomly stop by."

"I had a date."

"And I'm guessing it didn't go well?"

She shrugged. "It was fine…"

"Well, we were just about to eat. Hungry?"

"I already ate, but I'll take a beer."

Charlie was already halfway there, the cap gone. "Hey, Denise."

"Hey." She smiled at him.

He stared for a bit then turned back to the kitchen.

I stopped myself from rolling my eyes. Charlie was a ladies' man, but when it came to Denise, he was a schoolboy who had no game. It was the weirdest thing. "Let's sit." We moved to the table.

"So, Dax is really gone?" Denise asked.

"Yep. We're just friends."

"Man..." She shook her head. "You sure you know what you're doing? Because he was sooooo hot."

"Yes, I know." My girl downstairs would probably get mad at me pretty soon. "It wasn't right. I'm not angry at him anymore, but I just can't look past it."

"Yeah, I get it," she said. "There are other fish in the sea."

There were no fish like Dax, so I would probably be disappointed for a long time. "Yeah." We kept talking while Charlie cooked in the kitchen, and once he was done, he brought the plates to the table.

"You sure you don't want some, Denise?" Charlie asked.

"That's so sweet, but no thank you."

He sat down then ate, purposely not looking at her.

"How's work been?" I asked.

"It's alright," she answered. "Really hectic. My shifts go by so quickly because I'm hustling the entire time. I'm supposed to get a thirty-minute lunch, but I just eat quickly and get right back to it."

"That's terrible."

She shrugged. "I would just scroll through my newsfeed and waste time, so I'd rather be working since I'm there anyway. But when I get home, I sleep so hard." She shook her head. "Twelve hours sometimes."

"Understandable." I ate my tacos.

Charlie was already finished because he ate so quickly, scarfing down his food. "Nursing is a tough job. You've got to be resilient in a lot of ways to do it."

"Yeah." She shook her head slowly. "I've been doing it for years, but it still knocks the wind out of me."

"Working in the ER in a hospital in Manhattan is probably a totally different experience from working in Connecticut or something," Charlie said. "So you're in a fast-paced environment, with lots of different kinds of patients, working in a trauma center… It's gotta kick your ass most days."

"Oh, it does," she said with a laugh. "I'm off for the next four days…thank god."

"Want to come to our game tomorrow night?" Charlie asked. "We usually get dinner afterward."

"Yeah, that sounds like fun." Denise turned to me. "I only saw one of Carson's games in college, so it'll be nice to watch her kick some ass."

"I'm the only chick on the team, so I don't kick much ass," I said with a laugh. "I make a lot of shots, though."

"I'm in," Denise said. "Matt will be there?"

"Yeah." Charlie looked at his plate, as if he were forcing himself so he wouldn't look at her too much.

I was surprised he'd spoken to her as much as he did. That was new.

"What are you working on, Charlie?" Denise asked.

"A few things, actually. There's this historic building in Brooklyn they're trying to tear down. I'm covering that. There're a few other things here and there…" He drank his beer then cleared his throat. "My biggest article is about this new bar in Manhattan. Instead of throwing darts, they want to throw axes. It's supposed to be a lumberjack theme, but the city is trying to shut it down for safety reasons. But the bar says they have all the insurance for it, so it shouldn't matter."

"Wow," Denise said. "That sounds like a fun bar. Dangerous, but fun."

I watched them talk back and forth. I purposely withdrew from the conversation to see what would happen. Charlie made her laugh more than once, and he slowly became more confident.

It was like I wasn't there at all.

WHEN DENISE LEFT, Charlie carried the dishes to the sink and started to wash them, along with the pots and pans.

I walked into the kitchen and crossed my arms over my chest. "Okay, what the hell was that?"

"What?" He scrubbed the dish then set it on the counter.

I placed it in the dishwasher and waited for the next dish to be put away. "Don't *what* me."

"I was just talking to her."

"Yeah, but you were interesting and charming."

He scrubbed the next dish before handing it to me. "I'm always interesting and charming."

"Yeah, but never around her. You were finally yourself. What's up with that?"

He worked on the next dish and didn't say anything.

"Charlie?"

"Kat is still dating Nathan, so I thought…I don't know."

"You're gonna go for her?" I asked in surprise.

He turned off the faucet, dried his hands, and then turned to me, leaning against the counter. "Sometimes I think she could be into me."

"Because?"

"We ran into each other a while ago, and…I don't know. I can feel it."

I didn't tease him because this was important to him, but I didn't believe that. "Are you sure you're not projecting your feelings onto her?"

"Maybe. But you saw us at dinner. We click."

"Charlie, you just had a conversation. That's it."

"But we have chemistry. Just ask her—"

"I told you I'm staying out of this." I raised both hands. "Switzerland, alright?"

He crossed his arms over his chest. "I waited six months after our breakup to do anything, and Kat's seeing someone, so I think I'm going to go for it. I'm tired of waiting. I'm tired of going on dates just to get laid. I actually like Denise, so I should do something about it instead of doing nothing like a pussy." He got riled up quickly, like this had been bothering him for a bit.

"For the record, I never told you not to do anything. You made that decision entirely on your own."

"But I know the predicament it will put you in."

"Well...it's shitty. But if you feel this strongly, you can't just turn that off. You can't not do what you want to keep someone else happy. I mean, that's no way to live. And you have waited long enough, Charlie. I don't think it matters how long you do wait. It will hurt Kat either way."

He closed his eyes and sighed. "Does she still have feelings for me?"

I couldn't betray her confidence. "Even if she did, I would never tell you. If you're going to do this, you just need to figure out the best way to go about it."

"Which is?"

I shrugged. "I haven't got a damn clue, Charlie. There's really no answer here."

"Yeah..." He straightened and ran his fingers through his short hair.

"Denise may not even feel the same way, Charlie. So, I would figure that out before you do anything."

"Then ask her."

"How many times have I said I can't do that? I'm loyal to her, I'm loyal to you, I'm loyal to Kat... You're gonna have to do this on your own."

"What if I'm wrong, and she's not into me?"

"Then we pretend it never happened. And maybe it'll give you the closure you need to move on."

He took a deep breath. "I hope I don't need to move on..."

Selfishly, I wanted Charlie to drop his feelings because it was going to make my world extremely complicated if he didn't. I was going to lose someone at some point, and I couldn't cut out my sister or my roommate, so it would probably be Kat. But I didn't want to lose my best girlfriend. I didn't want her to be so hurt that she could never be around us again. I didn't want her to hate my sister or my best friend. I didn't want her to hate me for not telling her the truth. The odds of this going over well were slim, and I was really dreading that moment.

WE WALKED into the room with the court, all four of us.

Denise looked at the guys on the court, who were already doing their warm-up by taking shots and passing the ball. Most of them were shirtless, including Dax.

Oh geez...I forgot how hot he was.

Denise looked at me and then the court. "You're going to play against those giants?"

"Hey, I can hold my own pretty well," I argued.

"It's true," Charlie said. "She's quick on her feet."

Matt averted his eyes. "It's so hard not to stare..."

"Then don't not stare," Charlie countered.

"But I've got a man now," Matt said. "Seems wrong."

"Aww, that's cute," Denise said.

We moved to the bleachers and took a seat, putting down our water bottles and towels.

Denise sat beside me. "Is Dax here yet?"

"Over there on the court with the eight-pack, massive shoulders, and built chest." I said.

"And you're just going to play with him?" she asked incredulously.

"That's the plan."

She shook her head. "Good luck, girl."

Charlie stood up and took off his shirt—even though he'd never done that for a game before. He jogged onto the court.

Denise's eyes immediately went to his frame, watching him as he ran off.

Maybe Charlie was right.

Matt left his shirt on and moved onto the court.

"Are you going to take off your shirt too?" she teased.

"Nah. I've got class." I took a drink from my water bottle and made my way onto the court.

Dax had just finished greeting Charlie and Matt when he noticed me. Over six feet of sweaty muscles, he was perfect. His biceps and triceps were slick and shiny, and his carved stomach was like a washboard. He was easier to tolerate fully clothed. But this...this was rough.

His eyes lightened noticeably as he looked at me, and a slight smile moved onto his lips. He approached me, hands on his hips. "I'm glad you're playing with us. My team won the game last week."

"Because I wasn't here?" I asked playfully.

He shrugged. "It's an odd coincidence, huh?"

"Or maybe no coincidence at all." I nudged him in the side with a smile and got ready to play. "Let's do this."

We started the game, and Dax wasn't on me all the time. Sometimes other guys covered me, and they were definitely more aggressive, treating me like another guy instead of the five-foot-five woman that I was.

Charlie was on my team, so we always worked to get open for each other, to get the ball and send it into the hoop. Matt was on the opposite team, so whenever he was on top of me, he kept a respectful distance.

When I made a three-pointer, Denise stood up and screamed. "That's my girl!"

Charlie played harder than he ever had, dominating the court like it was life-and-death. He broke out in a heavy sweat, his skin shiny and slippery. His fit physique stole the show, his shorts low on his hips.

He was such a show-off right now.

When I got the ball again, Dax covered me.

I almost dropped the ball because the whiff of his cologne was too much, mixed with the scent of his sex. It gave me a sudden flashback of the last time we were together, and I broke concentration just for a second. It was enough to make me lose control of the ball.

But Dax didn't react right away, like he didn't want to steal it from me.

I got the ball again and dribbled away.

"I'm open!" Charlie ran back, ready to make a three-pointer.

I passed it.

He jumped in the air and made it. "Yes!"

Dax turned to me, his hands on his hips. "Your plan is working."

"Sorry?"

He nodded to Denise. "She's definitely paying attention to him."

WHEN THE GAME WAS OVER, we were all exhausted. Everything was sore, including my ass. My calves burned, and my lungs ached for air.

But Charlie walked it off like nothing happened. He strolled to the bench, dried off with a towel, acting nonchalant even though it was obvious to me he was still showing off. His abs were constantly flexed because he wouldn't relax whatsoever.

"I didn't know you were such a good player." Denise grabbed his water bottle and handed it to him.

"Thanks." He took it and sat down, keeping space between them, either because he was nervous or because he smelled like he'd just worked out.

"What about me?" I walked slowly, practically limping, and then dropped onto the bleachers, sighing because my entire body was sore. "Oh god, I'm gonna die." I grabbed the bottle and sucked on it like a baby on a nipple.

She chuckled. "You kicked ass too. But Charlie really stole the show."

He wiped his face with his towel. "I like to play hard."

Denise wasn't looking at me, so I rolled my eyes.

"Should we get something to eat?" Matt asked. "If I don't eat soon—"

"You'll die," Charlie said. "Yeah, we're aware of your strange condition."

Dax walked up to me after exchanging a few handshakes with his guys. "You okay?" He had a slight smile on his face, amused at my discomfort.

"My ass hurts." I set the bottle beside me and patted my face with a towel.

"Maybe it's because you're sitting on a steel bleacher."

"Nope," I said. "It's because Charlie made me hustle like it was the NBA Finals."

Dax grabbed his towel and patted his face dry before he rubbed it across his chest and shoulders, collecting all the sweat that dripped down that beautiful tanned skin.

I kept my eyes straight ahead and refused to let myself stare.

"We're gonna get pizza," Dax said. "You guys want to come along?"

Matt answered for all of us. "Yes. Please."

Dax chuckled. "Hungry?"

"He has a condition," Charlie said. "If he doesn't eat the second he's hungry, he dies."

Dax turned to me, still amused. "I'm pretty hungry too, so maybe I have that condition as well."

"Dude, let's go." Matt got up. "I need pizza in my stomach. *Pronto.*"

Everyone stood up—but me.

With his arms over his chest and the towel over his shoulder, Dax looked down at me, the blood making his skin flush a slightly red color, the same way he looked when we'd been screwing for a long time. "You aren't coming?"

"I think my ass is broken."

He grinned then extended a hand. "Come on."

I grabbed him, immediately felt his pulse, immediately felt that surge of excitement when I came into contact with him. But I didn't respond to it, buried that reaction deep down inside. I got to my feet then cringed.

"If it hurts now, it's really going to hurt tomorrow."

"Oh, I know." I grabbed my bottle and walked beside him.

Denise was up ahead with Charlie and Matt on either side of her.

"You need me to carry you?"

"I'd rather die."

He chuckled. "Proud woman."

"Damn right."

We headed outside then walked to the pizza place. His guys were farther ahead, while my friends walked behind. I was a little slow at the moment, so Dax decreased his pace to match mine.

"What's happening with Charlie and Denise?"

"He's going for it."

"Yeah?" he asked in surprise. "How do you feel about that?"

"If she's into him too, it's going to cause a lot of problems for me. So I'm not super excited about it."

"Did you tell him that?"

I shook my head. "I know how Charlie feels about her. I would never stand in his way."

"So, you think Kat won't be happy? Even though she's seeing Nathan?"

"No. Between you and me, Charlie was the love of her life. She and Denise are friends, so if Denise goes for it, it'll be a betrayal to Kat, and I'm stuck in the middle. Or Kat will realize I knew all of this and feel like I betrayed her. I'm just afraid this is going to end up with Kat and me no longer friends."

He looked ahead, turning heads as he walked past a group of women. But he didn't seem to notice them. "Yeah, that's a rough spot."

"They haven't been broken up that long either. If it'd been years, maybe it could work. But I can't expect Charlie to wait that long. And even if Kat doesn't get angry at me or Denise, she'll probably be so uncomfortable around the two of them that she'll just disappear."

"Yeah. No matter how it plays out, it doesn't have a happy ending."

"No." I shook my head. "If Charlie and Denise ended up together, that would be great because he would be my brother-in-law. He's always been my brother, but now he actually would be family. I'd be an aunt to his kids, related by blood. It'd be totally awesome. But...I don't know where Kat fits into that scenario."

"Yeah."

"Anyway, enough about the drama in my life..."

"I'm not sure if that constitutes drama," he said with a chuckle.

"It's pretty much a soap opera. What about you?"

He shrugged. "My sister has been seeing this guy for a while. I'm meeting him on Friday."

"Why is that drama? Please don't tell me you're going to be an obnoxious protective brother? That shit is so outdated."

He grinned in guilt. "I can't help it."

I rolled my eyes. "Just be nice. I'm sure he's great."

"Why?"

I shrugged. "She watched what you went through, right?"

He turned his gaze and stared at me for a while, his eyes a little soft. "Right."

"So, she'll be fine. Is he hot?"

"No idea what he looks like."

"What does he do?"

He shrugged.

"You don't know anything about this guy?"

"My sister is very protective of her privacy."

"Probably because she knows you'll rip apart anything she tells you."

He chuckled. "Yeah. Maybe."

I looked up ahead and stared at his friends. "So, do they know you're a billionaire?"

His mood soured slightly at the change of subject. "That'd be pretty hard to hide, wouldn't it?"

You hid it from me for five weeks. "I really have no idea."

"These are my buddies from high school. So, they don't really see me that way."

"Oh…then you've known each other a long time."

"Yeah. A really long time."

"Do you have rich friends?"

He nodded. "Some. I keep it separate. I prefer to keep my normal life as normal as possible. In that world, people are corrupt, greedy, and simply toxic."

"Really? I thought it would be all about shopping sprees with a little dog sitting in your Louis Vuitton purse."

He chuckled. "That's exactly how it is. But my friends on that side of the spectrum are a bit snobbish. All they want to talk about is money, who's made a deal recently, how to make more money, how to show off the wealth they already have. Even though they're in the top one percent, they're very insecure."

"If you grew up in that world, why are you so down to earth?"

He turned back to me, a slight smile on his lips. "Did you just give me a compliment?"

"What are you talking about? I always give you compliments."

"About how hot I am."

"Well, you are really hot. You want me to lie?"

He faced forward again, his smile wider. "Never."

"Come on, you're great."

"Yeah?"

"Yeah."

We reached the pizza place and sat at a big table. Dax took a seat with his friends, so I sat on the other side with mine. We ordered a couple pizzas, wings, and beers all around.

Matt kept drumming his fingers as he watched the staff serve other tables. He looked at the kitchen, as if he expected to see our order being made.

"Drink your beer and chill." Charlie grabbed the handle of his frosted mug and brought it to his lips for a drink.

"Why don't you eat before a game?" Denise asked.

"I did," he snapped. "I just have a fast metabolism."

"You're almost thirty, so I doubt it," I countered.

"Look, I just get hungry more often than most people," Matt said. "Jeremy thinks it's cute."

"Because Jeremy is getting sex from you," Charlie said.

"How is that going anyway?" Denise asked.

"Great." Now that Matt was distracted by the conversation, he stopped fidgeting. "We went to the movies the other night then went home and had sex. We kinda just fell into a relationship right away, which is new for me. I don't really do that."

"That's great," Charlie said. "I prefer you when you're settled down. You're calmer."

"Psh," Matt said. "I'm never—" He shut his mouth when he saw the wings being carried out. "Oh, thank god."

Denise chuckled then turned to Charlie. "What about you? Are you seeing anyone?"

Charlie had taken a sip of his beer right when she asked, so he continued to drink, like he needed a few seconds to compose himself after hearing the question. He drank his beer like water, and while he loved beer, he didn't love it that much. He set it down and licked his lips. "No."

I was starting to wonder if Denise was attracted to him, based on the limited interactions I witnessed. She and Kat were friends and I didn't picture her going after a friend's ex, but maybe she'd had a change of heart.

He cleared his throat. "You?"

"I went out with a doctor from the hospital, but it didn't go anywhere." She grabbed a few fries and wings and put them on her plate, looking dressed up to eat something so casual.

"Who wants to date a doctor anyway?" Matt asked. "Touching people all day long…"

"I touch people all day long," she countered. "Probably more than a doctor."

"Oh yeah, that's true." He devoured two wings in a few seconds then dunked his fries into his ketchup before scarfing those down too.

Dax watched him from his side of the table. "Feeling better, man?"

Matt had his mouth full, so he gave a thumbs-up.

Dax and his friends laughed.

I was eating as much as Matt, but I didn't make it as obvious.

Denise turned to me. "So, this isn't weird for you?"

"Meaning?" I took a bite of my fry, loving the crunch.

"You're hanging out with Dax like nothing happened." She kept her voice low so the guys on the other side of the table wouldn't hear.

"You mean, being grown and mature adults?" I asked sarcastically. "Relationships don't work out all the time, and the exes can be in the same room together. Look at Charlie and Kat. They're fine."

"Yeah, true," she said with a nod. "But you guys broke up a few days ago."

"We didn't break up," I corrected. "We were never really together in the first place. It was more of a fling."

"Maybe." She kept staring at me. "But you really liked him."

"I never said that." I just ate, keeping my cool.

"No," my sister said. "But it was obvious that you really liked him."

"Well, he ended up being a big fat liar, so that changed my feelings pretty quickly." I grabbed more fries. "Can we talk about something else now? Something interesting, preferably."

FIVE
DAX

I was on the phone in my office, talking to our overseas manufacturer. The worst part of my job was all the meetings. So much talking but so little productivity. If I said I was passionate about the software aspect of the company, I'd be lying. I was only passionate about my family's legacy.

My assistant popped her head in.

I gave her a glare because I was on the phone.

"The reporter from the *New York Press* is here."

I held up my finger to tell her I needed a few minutes.

She disappeared.

I finished up the meeting then picked up the phone to call her in. "Send her in." I hung up then got out of my chair to walk around my desk. My hands slid into my pockets, and I felt my heart pick up just a little bit. Being friends with Carson was easier than I expected it to be, but nothing could change my attraction to her. Her humor, her candor, the selfless way she cared about her friends.

The door opened a moment later, and my assistant let Carson into the room.

She was in a black dress and heels, her badge around her neck to identify her status at the most prestigious paper in the country. She had her notebook with her, tucked under her arm. Her brown hair was straight, and her green eyes had never turned hostile again after the conversation we'd had in this very room.

My eyes took her in, and time slowed down a bit because everything about her was irresistible to me. It wasn't just the way that tight dress fit her incredible body; it was the way she carried herself, the way she filled every room she stepped into with an undeniable presence. It was comforting but also authoritative, like she knew her worth and would never allow anyone to say otherwise.

Sometimes it was difficult to be around her because I suspected my feelings would never entirely go away. She would always be the one who got away, the woman who could have been something significant to me if the timing had been better, if I hadn't fucked it up with my stream of lies.

But at least I had some of her…a piece of her.

I walked over to her and felt my lips rise in a slight smile. "That meeting ran longer than I expected. Hope you didn't wait too long."

"It's fine. I know how it goes." She came closer to me but didn't embrace me. She would probably normally shake my hand if I were someone else, but that would feel out of place for us…since I'd kissed her everywhere. She moved to the couch and took a seat.

I sat across from her and rested my ankle on the opposite knee, my arm on the armrest.

She got her things organized.

I just stared at her, watched her put the recorder on the table and turn it on before she opened her notebook and got her pen ready. She crossed her legs and leaned back, lifting her gaze to look me in the eye.

It took me a second to process that look, to feel that eye contact and force myself to ignore the rush in my veins. Attractive women were a dime a dozen in this city, but they didn't look at me with those intelligent eyes, that sexy spunk. They didn't possess her fire, her drive.

It'd been a few days since I'd seen her. She was such a good player on the court, but she was also humble about it, admitting how sore she was from playing so hard. I spent my time having quiet evenings at home, working and ignoring the fake apartment I still had the lease on. "Your ass feeling any better?"

She smiled slightly. "It's still pretty sore."

"Those heels don't help."

"Yeah, but flats are out of the question."

"Why?"

"Just unprofessional."

"Wow. Didn't know the *New York Press* had such a strict dress code."

"They don't. I do." She turned the page in her notebook and clicked her pen. "You're fine with me recording you?"

"Sure."

"For this editorial piece, we're looking to understand the role of your family within the company, and the way your software has slowly affected millions of people and businesses. Your creation is all around us, from our phones to our laptops. Honestly, it changed the tech industry. Just want to better understand the family behind it because you've been notoriously private for decades."

But that privacy couldn't hide my disastrous divorce. "I have a question first."

"Go ahead." Her professional attitude wasn't much different from how she was on an everyday level, but she was definitely more soft-spoken, more focused.

"Anything going to happen with Denise and Charlie? I heard her ask him if he was seeing anyone."

"You heard that?"

And I heard Denise question Carson about the normalcy of our situation. I also heard her response, that we were just a fling that died out, that people could be mature and remain friends even when a relationship was over. It wasn't a fling to me, but I tried not to take it personally that it had been to her. "Yes."

She lost her confidence slightly, like she was embarrassed I'd probably overheard other parts of the conversation. "Yeah, I thought that was odd too. Charlie has asked me to feel her out before, to see how she feels about him, but I've always declined because it would feel like a betrayal to Kat. Now, I'm just curious to know how my sister feels about my best friend."

"I think there's a spark there."

"Yeah, me too. I feel like eighth graders talking about it."

"Like I said, drama." I smiled.

"It does feel that way. How does Nathan feel about Kat? Is he sprung?"

I didn't want to share what he'd told me in confidence, but I didn't want her to think Kat would definitely find her happily ever after. "He's into her, but not in love by any means."

"Well, they haven't been dating long."

"Yeah."

She looked down at her notes again. "Do you remember your grandfather well?"

"I have a lot of memories." My elbow pressed into the armrest, and my knuckles rested against my jawline. "He was brilliant. Just the way he spoke, he had this eloquence about him that conveyed how bright he was. In terms of development, I wasn't around much for that, can't recall his process. But when my father ran this place, he was really involved in the software aspect of the business. I think having several generations of people with a good understanding of the product as well as the business has allowed us to retain our success over so many generations."

"Are you that way too?" she asked. "Do you just handle the business side of things, or are you part of the development and expansion of the software."

"There're a lot of brilliant minds working for this company, and they're the ones evolving the program. I'm not involved with that process, but when I meet with the team, I focus on the applications of our new products and guide them into the kind of evolution I want to see. I see the big picture, but they see all the steps to get there."

"Two kinds of minds working together."

"That's a good way to describe it."

"There've been rumors that Clydesdale may be teaming up with one of the biggest American companies for a project. Is that true?"

My only response was a smile.

"Keeping secrets, huh?"

I shrugged.

She smiled and moved on. "Your sister is also a big player in the company?"

"She's head of distribution, but we work closely together. She's also involved in the big decisions of the company because she holds significant shares."

"And Rose Frawley?"

Just hearing her name made acid flood my mouth. "She's more of a silent partner..."

She studied my face, probably saw the venom enter my eyes. "I don't have to ask about her if you don't want me to. I can omit it from the article."

"It's fine," I said. "The world knows about my nasty divorce. It's no surprise."

She grabbed the recorder and turned it off. "How does that work anyway?"

"It doesn't. She just gets a check."

"Like, forever?"

I nodded. "I was an idiot who didn't get that prenup. Therefore, she owns half of what I own, which includes this business." I was so fucking stupid, so fucking naïve.

"Can you buy her out?"

I shook my head. "She won't sell."

"Why?"

"Why would she accept a big check now when she can collect for the rest of her life? Then her children can inherit that and continue to collect."

Her eyes fell in a deep look of sadness. "Jesus…"

"Yeah. It sucks." I'd had enough time to process what had happened, but it still haunted me. I was ashamed she'd made a fool out of me in front of the whole world, that she'd robbed my family of the profits from their hard work. If we'd just gotten a divorce decades down the road because of irreconcilable differences, it wouldn't hurt so much. But the fact that it was all a ploy, that she used me to get to this level, that when I suggested a prenup and she was offended, it was all a ruse. That's what fucking stung.

She took me for a ride.

I trusted too easily. I saw the good too easily.

Carson dropped her gaze for a moment and shook her head slightly. "I'm sorry, Dax. That's so shitty."

"Yeah…thanks."

"Maybe someday you can remedy the situation."

No. She got what she wanted, and she would never give it up. "Next question."

She sighed before she grabbed the recorder and turned it back on. "Where do you see this company in the next five years?"

"No idea. I hope it's still successful and customers still like our product. But I avoid thinking about the future as much. I focus on being the best I can be in the moment. If you work hard, there should always be a future. But what that future will be exactly is always unknown."

She made a note in response to what I said. "Do you plan to hand this company to your son one day?"

"Or daughter," I added.

Her eyes changed slightly, like that response meant something to her.

"I don't have a family and I'm not sure if I ever will, but if I do and they want it, of course. But my sister may want the same thing, and she's just as entitled to it."

"But you want it to stay in the family? You don't intend to sell or outsource a CEO?"

I shook my head. "No one is going to care about a company more than someone whose name is on the door. The best way to invest long-term success is to have someone who sees it as a legacy, sees that it's more than just money. So, no, I intend to keep it in the family as long as possible."

"And if neither you nor your sister has descendants?"

"She'll definitely have kids. Her dream is to be a mother."

"And is your dream to be a father?"

I studied her face, wondering if she was asking these questions for her article or for personal reasons. "Dream is too strong of a word. I'm open to the idea. When I was married, I always assumed we would have children. But now, I can't picture myself getting remarried, so I'm not sure how that would work."

She nodded but didn't make a note.

"What about you?"

She regarded me, an eyebrow slightly raised. "Meaning?"

"Do you want a family someday?" She used to be so closed off from me that I couldn't get a word out of her, but now that we were friends and her attitude was different, I could actually get to know her in a way I couldn't before. It was ironic that she was more giving after I betrayed her, but not before. My lies pushed her away, but once we weren't involved, she didn't see me as a threat anymore...so she shared her life with me.

"Not really. With my job, it's just not feasible. I'm put on assignments with twenty-four hours' notice, and then I'm gone for an extended period of time. Not sure what kind of life I could provide to a little person in that scenario."

"Well, there'd be a man in the picture, right?"

She shrugged. "If I were going to do the whole mom thing, I'd want to do it, you know? Not push it on my partner. But my sister will have kids, so I don't need to worry about it. Besides, being a fun aunt is way better than being a mom."

In the limited time I'd known her, it was obvious how passionate she was about her work. She took it seriously, like it was a calling rather than just a paycheck. "When did you know you wanted to be a journalist?"

"I've always known."

"Really?"

"Oh yeah. When I was in high school, I was the editor of my paper for four years in a row. When I graduated, it was at a time when newspapers were losing revenue and income as a writer was less realistic, but that didn't change my decision to pursue it. I knew I'd have to work even harder to get the job I wanted. But now I have it. Sure, ten years ago, I would be making twice as much, but that's just how it goes."

"What is it about the job that you're so passionate about?"

She considered the question for a long time.

"What would make you put your life on the line in Iraq? What would make you chase down a criminal in an alleyway?"

Her gaze turned back to me. "The truth."

I watched her eyes soften with sincerity.

"Preserving the truth of the world. Tell people what's really happening. Documenting it for generations to come. If I weren't sent to Iraq, all our information for that story would have come from other sources, which makes it biased. If you really want to get to the core of a situation, you need to witness it yourself. I know I'm not a doctor or a firefighter, but I think my job is pretty important. The media has the ability to completely dictate our way of life. It's pretty important…at least, I think so."

"It is important. It must be if you think your life is worth it."

She shrugged. "We're all gonna die sometime, right? Personally, I'd rather die young than when I'm old with some disease or inability to remember who I am."

"There's a lot of years in between that, though. The golden years can be a wonderful time...before the end."

"Maybe," she said noncommittally. "Enough about me."

"You're far more interesting than I am."

She rolled her eyes. "I'm not some sexy billionaire with the world at his feet..."

"That's not interesting. Boring, if you ask me."

She released a laugh. "If you're bored with a life in the fast lane, you're doing it wrong."

"Grass is always greener on the other side..." I'd been living this life a long time, and the older I became, the less it meant to me. I'd always been financially secure, while everyone else was out hustling for a better life, investing their time and energy into that dream. But since I was already there, I realized the things that really brought joy weren't tangible like money. Instead, it was conversations, connections, people. Spending time with Carson and her friends gave me a kind of simplicity that I found exhilarating. It was peaceful...easy. I wished I could have it again. "What else are you working on right now?"

"Just a few smaller pieces. You can't hit a home run every single time."

"Makes sense."

"You think I could get some photos that would reflect the family values of the company? Perhaps your childhood home? Something like that?"

"I grew up in the city, but we had a house in Connecticut where we spent a lot of time."

"Did you sell it when your parents passed?"

"Actually, no. It's still there. I just haven't visited in a long time." I felt ashamed to go back, not after the way I'd dishonored the family name.

"Well, is that something you're open to?"

I could have said no, but I didn't want to decline an opportunity to spend time with her. The world went still whenever we were together. Despite the disastrous way we ended, it felt like things were better now than they used to be. "Yes."

"Great. We'll take a drive. Maybe your sister can come along. I should interview her too."

"Not a bad idea."

She held her pen and scribbled notes into the notebook before she grabbed the recorder and turned it off.

"Can I ask you something?"

"Sure." She hooked the recorder on to the necklace around her throat before she closed her notebook.

"When did your parents pass away?" I felt like I could ask her anything I wanted, and instead of wanting to know less now that we weren't together, I wanted to know more.

"Pretty young. Denise and I had just become adults."

My father's death was still relatively recent, so it hurt all the time. "May I ask how they passed?"

She sighed. "Drunk driver."

"Wow...I'm sorry."

"Well, don't be too sorry because they were the drunk ones. They went to a party and had been drinking. Instead of calling for a ride or even calling me, they drove home and slammed into a telephone pole. Died on impact."

"Oh fuck." Now I felt terrible for asking, for putting her on the spot to share that with me.

"Yeah...it was rough. The telephone pole was new, and the road they took was a road they'd traveled on many times. But it was dark, and they probably didn't expect it to be there. It's just...yeah." She took a deep breath and let everything come out slowly. "No one else was hurt, thankfully."

I had no idea what to say to that, how to respond to such a traumatic event. Some might say it was her parents' own fault for choosing to drive under the influence, but that would be a cold way to put it. Carson and Denise were the victims of the whole thing, losing their parents in such a devastating manner. "I'm so sorry, Carson."

"Yeah...thanks." She gave a weak smile before she stood up. "I've got my sister, so I'm grateful for that."

"She looks nothing like you, but she's got your spirit."

She chuckled. "Nah, she's too sweet. She's like a sunflower, and I'm a rose covered in thorns. I can totally see why Charlie is hung up on her and calls me a hot mess all the time."

"Thorns can be trimmed...if you put the time in."

"But you're going to cut your hand in the process."

I rose to my feet, still taller than her despite her pumps. I smoothed out my tie and looked into her gorgeous face, finding her even more beautiful when she let herself be vulnerable for a rare moment. "Still worth it in the end."

I GOT to the restaurant first and ordered a glass of wine.

My sister hated it when I drank scotch. She argued it would kill my liver before I turned thirty-five.

But who needs a liver anyway?

I sat alone and waited, bringing the glass to my lips over and over, waiting for my sister to show up with the first man she'd ever wanted to introduce me to. The fact that it was his idea already made me like him. If he was pressing for the introduction, then he wanted to be serious, and that was all I needed to know.

I felt a hot stare on my face and shifted my gaze to the origin.

A woman sat at a table with a friend, and she held the stem of her glass as she gave me a slow smile. The eye contact was intentional, slightly playful.

I didn't let my gaze linger and quickly averted it.

I just wasn't in that place quite yet. I was a man with needs, but knowing Carson, she'd probably already hit up Boy Toy #1. Being around her only made it more difficult, because she was the person I wanted to undress, to kiss, to fuck. Knowing her on a deeper level made me want her more.

But there was nothing I could do about that.

I couldn't pursue her. I couldn't ask for more. I couldn't do anything to get her back.

She didn't want me, and even if she did, she wouldn't change her mind.

I had to get back on the horse at some point. Otherwise, my dick would explode.

But not now.

I saw Renee walk inside, a tall man behind her. He had dark-blond hair, a height that rivaled mine, and his blue eyes gave him a harmless look. When he gave the hostess a smile, he had a dimple in each cheek. It was a nice restaurant, so he wore a sport coat over his dark jeans. Renee was in a dark blue dress with her hair pulled back slightly, a few loose strands around her face.

Renee spotted me and approached the table. "Good. You ordered wine."

"I'm on my best behavior for you." I got to my feet, and even though we didn't greet each other with affection at the office or when she came by my place, I hugged her with one arm and rubbed her back.

"That makes me less nervous about this whole thing."

Her guy faced me and extended his hand, that genuine smile still there. "William."

I took his hand and gave it a firm shake. "Dax."

"It's great to meet you." He had a deep voice, with confidence in his gaze, but not arrogance.

I already liked the guy. "You too."

He pulled out the chair for my sister before he took the seat beside her.

My eyes were on him for a while, seeing the way he grabbed the wine list and scanned through the selection. "What are you drinking, Dax?"

"The 1994 LeMur."

"Wine connoisseur?"

"No expert, but I don't drink piss."

He chuckled. "I'll trust your decision. What about you, baby?"

She stilled at the affectionate name he threw across the table. "My brother picks out great wine, so I'll do the same."

I liked that he didn't change his behavior around me, that he wasn't being fake, that I could accept him as he was or dislike him for the same reason. It didn't matter to him. I'd never told Renee this, but I didn't want her to be with a man who bent over backward to gain the validation of someone else. He was secure in his true form.

When the waitress came over, they ordered their wine, and I got an appetizer because I was starving. It was a late dinner, and I hadn't had time to eat much for lunch.

Renee looked at her menu again. "I don't know what I'm getting..."

William eyed the menu. "The salmon looks good."

"That's what I'm having," I offered.

"Then it's settled." He set the menu down. "What about you? I know you hate fish."

"I think I'm getting the steak."

He smiled slightly, like he was amused by her choice.

When the waitress brought the drinks, she took our orders then left.

William took a sip. "Definitely a good choice."

Renee eyed us back and forth, clearly uncomfortable by the whole thing, like I'd challenge him to a duel or something. She was normally calm and collected, never uncomfortable even in the direst situations, but this was important to her, like she needed my approval even though she claimed she didn't.

I turned to William. "Baseball or basketball?"

"Basketball," he said immediately. "But I'll watch a game of baseball if it's on."

"I play in a basketball league with some friends. If you ever want to join, let me know."

"Wow, thanks for the invite. I'd love to pop in sometimes. My routine is the same every morning, and it gets old."

Renee eyed me with a raised eyebrow.

"That's exactly why I do it. Lifting weights to music is repetitive."

"I used to be runner, but that got too boring," he said with a chuckle.

"Competitively or as a hobby?"

"Competitively in college, but it became a hobby later. But it requires so much time to really put in the miles. It's much quicker to pump out a workout with weights."

"Definitely," I said. "When I was—"

"What is happening here?" Renee eyed me suspiciously.

My gaze turned back to her. "Meaning?"

"You aren't going to ask him where he went to college? What he does for a living? You're really going to talk about sports?" Renee spoke her mind in front of William, like it was eating her alive.

William smiled again before he took a drink of his wine, like her outburst was funny to him. "She's been anxious about this dinner all week…"

"Do you want me to interrogate him?" I asked incredulously.

"You're just…being weird." She lowered her voice as if William wouldn't be able to hear her even though he was right beside her.

"Renee, I don't give a shit where he went to college or what he does for a living. All I care about is the way he feels about you. If he's good to you and does right by you, that's all that matters to me. So, let me get to know him."

She dropped her gaze, like she was embarrassed by her outburst.

His arm moved around her shoulders, and he gave her a gentle squeeze. "She's just worried because she's crazy about me." He grinned as he looked at her, his hand rising to her hair and gently brushing it from her face. "Obsessed with me, really."

"Oh, shut up." She hit him playfully. "Am not."

"Sure, baby." He pulled his hand away. "Whatever you say…" His eyes lingered on her for a few seconds before he looked at me again, and those few seconds told me everything I needed to know about him.

He was the one crazy about her.

RENEE EXCUSED herself to the bathroom after dinner.

I watched her walk away before I turned back to him. "I'm not sure what she told you about me, but I'm not some crazy psychopath."

He was about to drink from his glass but stopped because he couldn't control the laugh that came from his lips. "She didn't say anything like that."

"It seems like it."

"We've been seeing each other for a while, and I suggested we all get together. She's met my parents."

"Really?" She didn't mention that to me.

"Yes. But trust me, she resisted. Of course, they loved her. Come on, why wouldn't they?" He drank from his glass. "But every time I suggested the two of us getting together, she kept sidestepping it, avoiding it, making excuses..."

I shook my head in disappointment.

"Look, I'm gonna be straight with you, man." He set his glass down. "I want this to go somewhere. I don't introduce just anyone to my parents. I did it pretty early on because I just knew. You know what I mean?"

Carson popped into my head. "Yeah, I do."

"So, I kinda pressured her into it. I think that's why she's so uneasy about the whole thing."

"Maybe she's not as serious about the relationship as you are." Maybe she wasn't ready for this. Maybe he forced their relationship to move too fast…just the way I did with Carson.

"No," he said with a chuckle. "Trust me, she's crazy about me. The problem is…she thinks so highly of you that she would be devastated if we didn't get along. You're all she has in the world. It makes sense."

My reaction didn't change, but I felt my heart soften inside my chest, felt the affection for my little sister grow. We were close, but not super close. We didn't actively spend time together outside the office, but it did feel like a parent-child relationship, where we were close but never quite friends. I looked a lot like our father, and I wondered if that was the way she saw me, as the man in her life outside her romantic relationship.

"I told her not to worry about it, but you know, she likes to worry…"

I didn't know this had been eating at her for so long.

"There's no reason to dislike me, and if you did, in time, you would come around. But that didn't ease her mind."

"Well, she should feel better now."

"We'll see," he said with a chuckle.

"Tell me more about yourself."

"Now you're going to interrogate me?" he asked with a smile.

"Share whatever you want to share with me."

"Let's see..." He swirled his glass before he took a drink. "I've got one brother. He lives in the city, and I'd say he's my closest friend. I'm close with my parents. Sorta have a helicopter kind of mom...if you know what I mean. So obviously, I wanted her to approve of Renee, but I wasn't worried she wouldn't. Wouldn't care if she didn't either."

I really liked this guy. Didn't take himself too seriously, he was easy to talk to, and he spoke highly about my sister in any context in which he described her.

"I'm a physician."

"What kind?"

"Cardiologist."

He didn't seem like the doctor type, so I was surprised.

"I like to fish, even though I don't go to the cabin very often. Too busy."

"Have any kids?"

"No. Never been married. I was in a long-term relationship in medical school, but we just grew apart." He shrugged. "And we were both too similar. It just didn't work. Renee is the first woman I've really dated since then, and that was like three years ago."

I could tell my sister was special to him based on everything he said, especially since he was the one to encourage meeting each other's families. "How long have you been seeing each other?"

"Six months."

I smiled slightly because my sister lied to me. She'd made it sound pretty new, but she was keeping her cards close to her chest, still unsure if she wanted me to meet him or not.

"What's with the grin?"

"My sister has been hiding this relationship for a long time."

He shrugged. "Yeah, she's a weirdo."

I chuckled. "Well, I'd like to get to know you better. As I mentioned, we play basketball on Wednesday nights. Will you be there?"

"Definitely. But how competitive is this?" he asked. "Because I'm decent but not amazing."

"Kinda competitive, but it's fine. We've got all kinds of players on the court." Including a small brunette who made up for her size with her ferocity.

"I'm down for a match."

"Great."

My sister came back from the restroom, and we left the restaurant, heading outside to the sidewalk to say goodbye.

William extended his hand and shook mine. "It was great to meet you, Dax. I think the two of us hit it off pretty well."

I nodded. "Yeah, I think we did."

His arm returned around her waist, and he looked down at her. "You can relax now."

She rolled her eyes.

"Well, goodnight." William prepared to turn away.

"Actually, do you mind if I take my sister home?" I asked. "Want to speak to her in private."

"Of course." William hugged her close then leaned down to kiss her. "See you later, baby." He turned around and walked up the sidewalk.

My driver pulled up to the curb, and I opened the door for her.

She eyed me before she got into the back seat.

I joined her, then we headed to her penthouse.

After a few minutes of silence, she spoke. "So?"

"I like him, Renee. But that's not what I want to talk about."

"Oh?"

"William made it sound like you're dragging your feet in this relationship."

Her eyes narrowed on my face. "He told you that?"

"A lot of things were said."

"I was gone for five minutes."

"We both get to the point. Another reason I like him."

"What is your point, Dax?" She crossed her arms over her chest.

"I just want to give you some advice. If you like this guy, you're serious about him, don't guard your heart. Don't keep your walls up. Be honest. Because anything less might jeopardize what you have."

She turned her gaze out the window.

"He really cares for you, Renee. It's easy to see."

"He loves me..."

"Yeah, I can tell."

She turned back to me. "After everything you went through with Rose...I guess I'm scared."

"If someone intends to deceive you, no amount of paranoia will allow you to see it before it's too late. The people who try to use you and manipulate are actors. They'll trick you, and as terrible as it is to say, there's nothing you can do to stop it. But if you continue to keep your walls up at all times, you'll stop everyone from getting to you, both good and bad. I don't know him well, but he seems like the real deal."

"He is."

"Then you shouldn't care what I think, Renee."

She rolled her eyes. "I can't help it, okay? I don't have a father to walk me down the aisle. I don't have a father to grill a man I bring home for Christmas. You're all I have." She looked out the window again. "Your opinion means a lot to me, and since it's just the two of us, I want you to be close to the man I marry."

I digested those words. "Is this a man you think you'll marry?"

She nodded. "I love him."

I'd only seen them together once, and I could picture them ending up together. William wore his heart on his sleeve, so I could watch it beat for my sister—right at the dinner table. "I'm sure I will be, Renee. You're so smart. You know how to pick the good ones from the bad ones."

"But you're smart too..."

Not smart enough.

"I really hated Rose, even when you were together, and I felt like it put a wall between us. I don't want that to happen again with the man I decide to be with."

My past would continue to haunt me forever. It affected every relationship I ever had, sabotaged my relationship with the woman who really blew my mind. "It won't. Nothing will ever stop us from being close. Rose was the biggest mistake of my life, and I won't repeat it. I've learned from my stupidity. You could never lose me."

She turned back to me, her eyes soft, a little wet. "You really like him?"

"Why would I invite him to basketball if I didn't?"

For the first time that night, she relaxed. She finally took a breath and let her shoulders fall.

"Now that I know how you really feel about him, I'll do what I can to bond with him. I can't force a relationship if the chemistry isn't there, but I think he and I are compatible. Don't worry about it."

She nodded. "Well...I'm glad we had this talk."

"Yeah, me too."

The car stopped in front of her penthouse.

She looked out the window before she turned back to me. "I really miss Mom and Dad. When I see William with his parents, it makes me sad."

I hated seeing my sister in pain, seeing the sadness I couldn't fix. "Me too."

"I know we aren't super close, but I'd like to be."

I hadn't put in much effort, because I'd been too busy fighting Rose and dealing with the depression afterward. I hadn't been emotionally available until I met Carson in that bar. That was the moment I was ready to feel something. "I would too, Renee."

SIX

CARSON

I was in the booth alone, drinking my glass of wine, when Denise walked in wearing her light blue scrubs and joined me. Her hair was curled but slicked in a short ponytail, and after working a twelve-hour shift, she still looked crisp.

"I'm so jealous of your work outfit."

She laughed. "Baggy clothes covered in people's germs?"

"Uh...let's skip the hug."

"That's what I thought." She got the waitress's attention and ordered a beer. "I would love to get cute every day for work. Dresses, skirts, heels...that's the one thing I dislike about my job."

"It gets old. You have to pick out what you're going to wear the night before...too much work."

"That's why I try to look good outside of work, because I don't get the opportunity often."

The waitress brought the drink and walked away.

"Are you still writing that editorial piece on Dax?" She took a sip.

"Yeah. We do mostly hard-hitting news, but people don't always want to read about scandals, wars, crimes against humanity. Sometimes they just want a good story. The history of his company is interesting. It's rare for a Fortune 500 company to remain a family company for so long. It has the corporate power but also the quaintness of a family-run business."

"And that's just...totally normal?"

I knew what point she was trying to make. "Honestly, it's been really nice. I like being friends. When we were fooling around, I felt like I didn't really know him, and not just because he was lying to me at the time. Now, I actually know who he is, and there's no pressure, so...it's easy."

"It's because you aren't risking anything."

"Maybe," I said with a shrug.

"But those old feelings? They just went away?"

"Uh, no," I said with a laugh. "I still want to jump his bones sometimes. But those feelings I had when we were seeing each other are gone. His betrayal kinda erased all that."

"But you don't seem mad at him anymore."

"I'm not one to hold a grudge." I ended the relationship, and he accepted that. No point in living in the past anymore. He shouldn't have lied to me, not when I was so scarred, but I understood his reasoning and didn't hate him for it. He was still a good person in my eyes. He wasn't a heartless, lying son of a bitch like my ex-husband.

"I guess that's good. He seems like a good guy. Maybe you two can try again later."

I drank from my glass and smeared my lipstick onto the edge. "No."

"Then you are holding a grudge."

"No. It's just that kind of trust is broken. That's all."

"Well, I don't see how you can be friends with someone if you don't trust them, and you seem to be good friends already."

"Not the same thing."

She shrugged then took a drink.

"I'm surprised you're pushing for him when he lied to me. I mean, I'm your sister." Shouldn't she be pissed off like an angry mob? Shouldn't she want to knee him in the balls?

"I'm not saying what he did was okay, but I get where he's coming from. It would get old trying to find someone to be with when your wealth is always the main focus of conversation. He could date women just as wealthy, but I imagine they're snobby and lazy. No, he shouldn't have lied as long as he did, but..." She shrugged. "He still seems like a sweetheart to me."

"He is." The comment was automatic because those feelings were undeniable. He'd always been good to me, protective in the alleyway and on the court, and supportive of my ambitions.

"Charlie is a sweetheart too, and those kinds of men don't grow on trees." She picked up her glass and brought it to her lips for a drink, her eyes scanning the bar.

I stared at her with my fingers wrapped around my glass, trying to read her body language, dissect the casual words that came out of her mouth. I wanted to shut my mouth and keep my distance because getting involved would no longer make me Switzerland, but the curiosity was too much. "You got a thing for Charlie?"

She turned back to me. "All I said was he's a sweetheart."

My eyes narrowed. "You didn't answer the question."

She rolled her eyes. "Saying a guy is a sweetheart doesn't mean—"

"Bitch, just answer the question."

She suppressed the smile on her lips, her eyes playful, just the way they used to be when we were kids. I could read her so well because I'd spent a lifetime doing it. The corner of her mouth lifted when she lied. "I may find him easy on the eyes..."

So, my mind wasn't playing tricks on me.

"Come on, watching a bunch of hot, shirtless guys play basketball is kinda irresistible."

"But Charlie is the only one you noticed."

"Well...look at him. He's fitter than an ox. How do you live with him and not hook up all the time?" She turned back to me. "Do you?"

"God, no." I held up my hand. I stuck out my tongue because the thought was truly disgusting. "Ew. Just ew."

"Ew? How can that possibly gross you out?"

"He's like a brother to me."

She shook her head. "But the very first moment you met him, you must have found him attractive."

"Eh. I'm not into blonds."

Her eyes narrowed. "Thanks..."

"I'm just saying, I prefer men who are a little darker."

"Like Dax."

"Exactly." Man, he was hot. "So, if you're into Charlie, are you going to go for it?"

"What?" she asked incredulously. "Are you crazy?"

"Why is that crazy?"

"Uh, hello? Kat?"

Trust me, I hadn't forgotten about her.

"I know she's more your friend than mine, but I would never do that to her. She's still hung up on him. That would be so terrible to break her already-broken heart like that."

I appreciated the sensitivity. But now I knew they both wanted the other...and they couldn't be together.

"Besides, Charlie might not even see me that way. If he sees you like a sister, he might see me the same way."

I had to hold back my chuckle so it wouldn't fly out of my mouth. Wow, my sister was oblivious. How did she not see the way Charlie stared at her pretty much every second they were together? "How long have you felt this way?"

"Only recently. That basketball game really had an impact."

It had been smart of Charlie to invite her.

"I thought maybe we could just hook up. You know, a one-time thing, but if Kat ever found out…that would be bad. And just getting into bed with him is a betrayal and would put you in a difficult situation."

I was already in a difficult situation.

"So, I should just forget about it. There are plenty of other fish in the sea, right? Dax is pretty hot, so maybe—"

"Uh, excuse me?" I snapped. "Bitch, he's off-limits."

She grinned. "Yeah?"

"I just mean, because he's technically my ex."

"Sure, Carson. Whatever you say."

CHARLIE WAS MAKING dinner when I walked inside. "Hungry?"

"Come on, are we really going to do this?"

He shook his head and kept cooking.

I sat at the kitchen table and scrolled through my phone as I waited for my personal chef to deliver my meal. We had a nice setup. I paid for all the groceries, and he did all the cooking.

He set the grilled chicken with rice and vegetables in front of me. "What's new with you?"

"Nothing."

He sat down and slid a fork toward me. He started to read his phone, elbows on the table and his body hovering over his food.

I stared at him as I ate, unsure what to do. If I told Charlie what Denise told me, what would happen? Would he leave the apartment and head to her place right now? Would they shack up right away? Why did I have to be in the middle of this?

"You're quiet."

"Just tired."

"You're never tired."

"Come on, that's impossible."

"Well, you're never tired when you eat."

I continued to stab the fork into the meat and vegetables, placing each bite into my mouth.

Charlie lifted his head and stared at me.

"What?"

"You're being weird."

"No, you're being weird. Who says someone's being weird?"

"Whatever." He turned back to his food.

I ate in silence, wishing I could talk to him about my dilemma. He was my best friend, the person I talked to about everything...but now, I couldn't say a word to him.

DAX WAS busy at the office all week, so his only availability was Saturday. He told me to meet him at his place and we would drive together. He texted me the address, and I walked a few blocks until I made it to Fifth Avenue... where all the fancy-pants people lived.

I checked in with the bellman and then the security guard before I was allowed into the elevator. It rose up the building then came to a gentle stop before the doors slid open and revealed a gorgeous living room with fresh flowers in vases, interesting paintings hanging around the space, a massive TV on the wall with enough couches to seat twelve people comfortably.

He really was a billionaire.

I stepped inside and heard the doors shut behind me.

He was nowhere in sight. "Uh...hello?" The backdrop of the living room was floor-to-ceiling windows that provided a gorgeous view of Central Park. There was a large dining table that could fit ten guests. He also had a full kitchen with a large island. It was a dream house, the kind of penthouse you saw in *People* magazine because a famous person owned it.

Footsteps sounded on the hardwood a moment later. Dax stepped out of the hallway in jeans and a classic tee, dressed in dark colors that complemented those dark eyes and hair. His scruff was gone, so it gave him an entirely different look, a clean look. Over six feet tall with the shoulders of a soldier, he was far more beautiful than the view of the park out of his windows.

He walked up to me. "Want anything to drink?"

If I spoke right away, I would stutter, so I let the silence pass for a few seconds before I cleared my throat. "No thanks. So...this is your place? A lot nicer than that other one." It wasn't a jab at his lie, but it was such a contrast, to see where he actually lived, where he ate and slept, brought his other dates.

"Want a tour?"

"How big is it?"

"Like ten thousand square feet."

"Jesus Fucking Christ." I blurted that out uncontrollably and covered my mouth at my lack of class. I was on the job right now.

He chuckled at my reaction. "It's fine."

"Yeah, let's skip the tour."

"Alright." He grabbed his wallet and keys off the counter.

It was weird to see him in that penthouse, to see who he was really was. But it also fit him a lot more than that fake apartment ever did. The suits he wore in his office fit him better than his t-shirts did. He'd always been a man with a powerful presence...and now it all made sense.

We returned to the elevator and rode down to the garage.

He stood with his muscular arms by his sides, his gaze straight ahead. "How's it going?"

"Good. You?"

"It's Saturday, so I'm happy."

"Well, you're working this Saturday."

"Nah. This isn't work." The doors opened to the garage, and he led the way. It was lined with Bugattis and Ferraris. They must belong to the tenants in the building, a collection of toys they probably never used because they had private drivers.

He walked to a black Bugatti, and the doors immediately unlocked when we drew near.

"This is what we're driving?" I asked in surprise.

"Yep." He opened the passenger door for me.

"Whoa. I've never been in one of these."

"Now you will. And you've been warned…I drive fast."

"Good." I sat down then looked up at him. "Why would you own this car if you didn't?"

He smiled then shut the door before he joined me. The engine roared to life with power, and then he was out of the garage and onto the road, headed for the tunnel to get out of the city. The roads and sidewalks were busy with people, but once we got out of the chaos, he could really floor it.

I examined the dashboard and felt the leather seats. "I feel like a race car driver."

"You got a license?"

"Yes."

"I'll let you take it for a spin later."

"You don't have to do that."

"I'm not doing it for you. I want to watch a sexy woman push my girl to the limit." He kept his eyes on the road and pulled off the flirtatious comment with no effort. One hand was on the wheel, while the other rested on the console between us. He was definitely in his element, a sexy billionaire behind the wheel of one of his toys.

"Do you have others?" I dealt with rich people all the time and had never met one who didn't own at least two fancy cars.

"A few."

"Are they in the garage?"

"One is. The other is at my place in the Hamptons." Now he'd put himself on display entirely, sharing his life with me freely, not censoring anything. It didn't seem like he was showing off his ridiculous wealth, just being honest.

"Is it on the beach?"

"Yep."

"So, you've got two places on the beach?" I asked.

"Well, this place actually belonged to my parents, so I wouldn't call it mine."

"But you inherited it."

"Technically, Renee and I both inherited it. The plan was to sell it and split the cash. But neither one of us want to sell it. So, it just sits there."

It was sweet that they cared more about their parents' legacy than money. "Do you visit often?"

"I haven't been since they passed away."

"Oh...I didn't realize that."

"It's fine." He kept his eyes on the road. "It doesn't matter how much time has gone by, it still hurts. The seasons change, but the scar on my heart never fades. But to avoid thinking about them or not going to my childhood home so I don't have to feel that pain...it would be like trying to forget them. I certainly don't want to do that."

"Yeah..."

We made it through the tunnel and eventually onto the open road. He got on the freeway and pressed the gas hard, pushing the car far beyond the speed limit.

"Oh my god, we're going so fast!" I raised my hands in the air even though the top wasn't convertible. "What are we at?" I leaned over the center console to see the dashboard.

"One twenty." He grinned, still driving with one hand.

"Wow, it's so smooth. But you're going to get a ticket."

He shrugged. "I don't care."

"Woo-hoo!" I waved to all the cars we passed as he weaved in and out of traffic.

"Wow, you really are fearless."

"No. I just don't get scared."

He kept going, moving farther away from the city so the highway was more open. It was incredible that we were pushing the car at such an intense speed, but the car remained so smooth, absorbing all the bumps in the road and gliding like a plane in the open skies.

I got comfortable in the leather seat and looked out the window, watching the landscape pass by, the tall trees and vegetation that were absent from the city. The only landscape available near me was the occasional park. The rest was all skyscrapers, sewer grates, and fire hydrants.

I loved the city. But I also loved the wide-open spaces.

He broke the silence. "What's new with you?"

"Well, I found out my sister has the hots for Charlie."

"No surprise there." He grinned. "He was dominating that court like he was about to get drafted into the NBA."

"But she said she knows she can't, because of Kat."

"Did you tell Charlie?"

"No."

"Why not? He's your best friend."

"And she's my sister. I'm so well connected to everyone that I can't be loyal to one person without being disloyal to another."

"If the guy has been into her for so long, I still think a heads-up would be nice..."

"And then what?" I asked. "He asks her out? We just forget about Kat?"

He sighed as he considered my questions. "I know the situation is complicated, but sometimes we all just need to be mature about things we aren't happy about and accept them."

I glanced at him, wondering if that statement applied to himself and our breakup.

"Maybe Kat needs to learn to accept this."

"That's a little harsh since she's still in love with him."

"No offense, but that's not Charlie's problem. Maybe seeing him move on will help her move on."

"Or just rip her apart..."

"What if Denise and Charlie are perfect for each other? Like, get married someday perfect for each other? But it never happens because of a relationship that's been over for months? That doesn't sound right. If Charlie just wanted some ass, this would be a stupid idea, but from what he's told me, she's the real deal."

"Yeah, I know." I wanted him to be happy. I'd never seen him feel this way about someone before. Women were a dime a dozen. They were there just to keep the sheets warm. He was happy with Kat, but he never talked about her the way he spoke about Denise. And if there was a chance for him to have that, of course, I wanted it to happen.

"Maybe you should talk to Kat."

"I...I don't know."

"You have to start somewhere. Because these two people not being together because of this other person sounds unfair."

"Well, Denise said she had the hots for Charlie, would do a one-night stand if Kat weren't a problem, so I'm not sure if she actually has real feelings for Charlie or if she just wants some D."

"I guess that does make a difference. But I think you should tell Charlie. It sounds like, no matter what you do, there's going to be drama, so you may as well put everything on the table."

"Maybe you're right."

"I'm always right. Wise beyond my years."

"Yeah...okay." I rolled my eyes.

He slowed the car down once he approached a property secured by a large gate with iron bars. A brick wall surrounded the area, masked by the trees and bushes that discreetly hid it from view of the road. He pulled up to the security keypad and typed in a code.

The doors slowly swung inward, revealing a paved road that led to a two-story house with unobstructed views of the water.

"Wow, this place is beautiful."

He drove forward down the path. There was grass on either side and, along the edges, blooming hydrangeas in colors of blue and purple. There were pink roses too, deep green bushes, and tall oak trees that cast shadows across the lawn. He parked at the entrance to the garage and killed the engine.

"Not a bad place to grow up."

"Yeah, it could have been worse."

We left the car and walked to the rear, where a large backyard with a lawn and a stone deck stretched before us. Patio furniture was outside, under the big umbrellas, and there was a gorgeous view of the water, the sound of the waves loud because they were only feet away.

"Do you mind if I take pictures?"

"No."

I pulled out my phone and snapped some shots.

"Pictures taken on a phone are good enough for the *New York Press*?" he teased.

"Honestly, these cameras are just as good as those big ones—and not as heavy."

He slid his hands into his pockets and stood in the sun, looking even sexier under the natural light, his eyes taking in the landscape of his childhood home.

I watched him for a moment, knowing he had no idea I was looking at him. "Did you have birthday parties out here?"

He snapped out of his thoughts and turned back to me. "My sister had tea parties out here on the weekends when she was young. The girls would get all dressed up with big hats and have tea and sandwiches."

"What about you?"

"Squirt gun fights." He grinned. "My birthday is in the summer."

"Oh, when?" It was summertime now.

He didn't answer and turned to the back door. He pulled out his keys and opened the double French doors that led to the house.

"Why aren't you answering me?" I followed behind him.

"Because I know you."

"What does that mean?"

"I know you'll make a fuss over it."

"Will not." I followed him into the house, seeing the living room with the white couches, the artwork of seashells and sandy beaches. There was a gray rug underneath. The rest of the house was in the same style, like a beach cottage. "Come on, tell me."

He moved forward into the dining room, where the family portraits were. "Fine." He gripped the back of one of the dining chairs and looked at me. "Saturday."

"As in, a week from today?" I asked in surprise.

He nodded. "Turning thirty-one."

"You got plans?"

He shrugged. "The guys will probably want to go to a club or something."

"The guys?" I asked. "As in Jeremy and Nathan, or billionaire guys."

"Billionaire guys."

My eyes narrowed on his face. "That's why you were at the same club that night, huh?" He'd come to my rescue when I least expected it, and he'd been dressed in a nice suit.

He held my gaze and didn't blink. "Yeah." He turned to the wall where the family portraits were.

I came to his side and looked at the pictures of his family, his grandparents on the far left, his parents' wedding photo, and a few of Dax and his younger sister. "You were so cute when you were little." I examined a picture of him when he was a teenager, maybe fifteen. I looked at other pictures, seeing him grow into a young man with a college diploma. "Must have broken a lot of hearts on the way..."

"Not proud of it."

I looked at the photos of his sister. "She's beautiful. Looks just like your mother."

He nodded in agreement. "She does."

"You look like your father...but a little like your mother."

"Yes. They were good people." He stared at their wedding photo. "My grandparents came from California. My grandfather was a fisherman and got a job at the docks. But he was also a genius, working on computers at night. No college degree."

"I love stories like that—the American dream."

"Yeah."

"Do you have aunts and uncles?"

"I do, but they're in California. They send a Christmas card every year, but we aren't close."

"Your mother's wedding dress is beautiful. Do you think your sister will wear it?"

"Not sure. She's never talked about it."

"Is your sister married now?"

He shook his head. "Not yet. But it won't be long."

"What does that mean?" I held up my phone and took a few pictures.

He turned to the kitchen and grabbed a couple glasses and filled them with water from the fridge. He carried them back outside to the patio. It was a beautiful summer day, a slight breeze in the air, and the waves were ferocious.

I followed him and joined him at the table. "Do you do that a lot?"

"What?"

"Leave the room without answering a question."

He took a drink and licked his lips. "I answer questions when I feel like it." He gave me a gentle smile, telling me he was teasing me. "My sister has been seeing this guy for a while, and I met him the other night."

"What did you think?"

"Good guy. He's playing basketball with us this week, actually."

"Oh, so you really like him."

"I don't know him well enough. But I can tell he's in love with my sister, and that's all that really matters to me." He took a drink. "I think she was afraid to introduce us because she feared I wouldn't like him."

"I hope you don't do the stupid older brother macho bullshit thing?"

He chuckled. "No. I guess she just really values my opinion." He stared into the glass for a while. "At the end of the night, we spoke in private, and she basically told me that it's important to her that I be close with her future husband since Mom and Dad are gone. When I was married, I was really distant because I was in a dark place. Without realizing it, we drifted apart. She's afraid the same thing will happen. Made me realize how much that divorce ruined me, affected all my relationships, even my relationship with you." He lifted his gaze and looked across the yard. "My sister has a strong spine, she's a tough woman, so I didn't realize how much she needed me. I didn't realize how alone she felt. She wants to bring our family closer together, so she didn't want me to meet him for as long as possible."

"That's sweet..." My eyes softened. "What's he like?"

"He's good-looking, likes sports. He's a cardiologist. He was the one that insisted on meeting me. That told me he was serious about her. He seems laid-back and confident, which I like. He didn't bend over backward and kiss my ass. No performance, no humble bragging."

"And you don't want your sister's boyfriend to kiss your ass?"

He shook his head. "I want her to be with a man who doesn't give a shit what anyone thinks of him."

I smiled. "That's really nice."

"He didn't seem to change his behavior around me either. He called her baby. He teased her. Stuff like that."

"What would you have done if you didn't like him?"

He rested his hand on top of his glass. "Nothing."

"Really?"

"I don't have to like him to respect her choice. Now, if he were some abusive jerk, that's a totally different story. But that's pretty hard to pick up on during an initial meeting. But I don't think that will be a problem with William."

"Is this the first boyfriend you've met or something?"

He nodded. "Other than high school boyfriends, yes. You know, the first serious one. And she told me she sees herself marrying him, so I think he's the one."

"Does she seem happy?"

"She was such a nervous wreck at dinner that it's hard to tell, but I'd imagine so." He drank from his glass and continued to look across the yard.

"I'll interview her next. See what she dishes about you."

"She'll take my secrets to the grave." He gave me a slight smile.

"You have secrets that need to be taken to the grave?" I teased.

"A real man always has secrets."

"Care to share?"

He chuckled and let his gaze wander across the yard. "Alright...but you're going to judge me for this."

"I really doubt it. I'm not a judgmental person."

"When I was in college, I had a fling with one of my mother's friends. Renee caught me."

"Whoa, what?" I straightened in the chair and cupped my mouth. "You did not."

"She was younger than my mom, obviously," he said with a chuckle.

"But she wasn't twenty."

"No...more like thirty-five."

I laughed. "Did your mother ever find out?"

"Nope. Renee never told her."

"What if she had?"

He shrugged. "My mom probably would have cut that woman out of her life."

"Do you still see her?"

"Last time was at the funeral. But she's in her forties now and married."

"Wow. I guess she taught you a few things."

"Actually, yes."

He was good at fucking, and he must have learned it somewhere.

"Quite a secret, huh?"

"Yeah. I'm impressed."

"You got any secrets? Something you haven't even told Charlie?"

"Wow…we're having this conversation while drinking water."

He relaxed back into the chair, his elbow propped on the armrests. The shade of the umbrella covered us both, and it was a nice color on him, making his tanned skin seem even darker. His fingers rubbed across his temple as he glanced back at the house. "My father used to collect scotch, but I'll never get us home safe if I open his storage."

"True. We'll stick with the water."

"Now, tell me."

I grinned in embarrassment, unable to believe I was going to share something I'd never even told my best friend. I didn't tell Kat or Denise either. "So, you know I kinda have this casual relationship with the mafia?"

"Yes." His eyes narrowed at the serious subject matter.

"Well, they had this big get-together at one of their restaurants, and they invited me. I met one of their guys, and we hit it off. We saw each other for a couple weeks, but when he became too attached, I ended it."

"You slept with a guy in the Italian mob?"

I nodded.

"And Charlie doesn't know?"

"Oh, he'd kill me. My sister would too."

"So, I'm the only person in the world who knows."

"Yep."

"You really are fearless." He gave me an incredulous look, but it was filled with a hint of affection.

"Look, I don't want a boring funeral. I want people to talk about my fling with the Italian mob, the fight I had with an Iraqi soldier, how I kicked some guy's ass in an alleyway. I want my death to remind everyone how much I lived."

He stared at me for a long time, letting those words sink in. "I respect that. But that also means you plan to tell people about this affair."

"Someday...but not anytime soon."

"And how was it with the guy?"

"The sex?" I asked, surprised he'd ask.

"Yeah. Is having sex with a criminal different from with a law-abiding citizen?"

"In general, it was definitely more aggressive, but more passionate because he's an Italian man with a sexy accent. But best sex I've ever had? Not necessarily. This was right after my divorce, so I was being reckless, more than usual, at least."

His fingers rested under his chin as he leaned my way slightly and watched me. "Then, is the best sex you've ever had with a porn star?"

"Can't say I've had the pleasure of bedding a professional..."

"Prince of Wales?"

I chuckled. "No. I asked him out, but he shot me down."

He grinned. "Biggest mistake of his life."

"Well, he's married, so he made the right choice."

"Ask out a lot of married guys?"

I knew how shitty it was to be cheated on, so I would never do that to another person. I'd had some really sexy guys come on to me, but their wedding rings were such a turn-off I wanted to throw up. "Never. Not my thing."

"Me neither."

I turned my gaze and looked across the yard, at the pink rose bushes under one of the oak trees.

He stared at me.

I could feel his look, so I shifted my gaze back to his.

His fingers brushed across his chin. "I've been with some incredible women, but you're the best I've ever had." He said the words simply, without a hint of hesitation, like my discomfort meant nothing to him.

I didn't know what to say, so I stared back, my heart picking up in response to his words. He was the best I'd ever had too, but I refused to say it out loud. A part of me didn't believe what he said, that it was just a line, but now that a relationship was off the table, there was no incentive to give me false praise.

"I'm not in the Italian mob and I've never held a gun, so I'm probably not the most exciting lover you've ever had—"

"Shut up, you know you are."

He didn't smile in triumph. His eyes remained serious, his fingers stilling against his chin. "Really?"

"Hands down." I wasn't sure why I told him that. I didn't owe him anything. I could have kept that secret, but now that the gates were open, I shared everything with him, without hesitation.

"That's quite the compliment."

"Well, you've got a nice dick."

A slow smile spread across his lips. "Wow, that's an even better compliment."

"People who say size doesn't matter, that it's all about the way you use it, are full of shit. Both matter—size and experience." I held up two fingers. "You've got both."

"This keeps getting better and better. No constructive criticism?"

It was perfect every single time. I missed it sometimes...all the time. "Nope. What about me?"

He released a quiet laugh. "No. You're perfect."

"If I was so perfect, my husband wouldn't have cheated on me." The bitterness escaped my voice when I'd meant to make a joke. But that pain was still there, right around my heart and lungs. I looked away, immediately regretting what I'd said the moment I said it. I hated being vulnerable, showing my weakness and handing out a map of my scars.

He stared at me and didn't say anything.

I drank from my water and waited for the moment to dissipate on its own, fly away with the summer breeze.

"Your husband's infidelity had nothing to do with you." He spoke with a strong voice, making his simple statement resonate.

"You didn't know our relationship."

"Doesn't matter. There are people out there who will always be unfaithful. It doesn't matter how amazing their partner is. They can't resist temptation, can't stop chasing the next hot thing on the block. It might seem like they're having a good time, but in reality, they're eternally unhappy. Nothing is ever good enough."

I turned back to him.

"So, feel bad for him. Not yourself."

"I don't feel bad for myself." I wasn't having a pity party.

"You're still carrying some kind of guilt, like you were the reason the marriage failed." He shook his head. "Trust me, it was him, not you."

"You don't know me that well."

He gave me a slight smile. "I know about your dirty secret with the mafia. That's gotta count for something."

A small smile moved onto my lips.

"And I know you a lot better now as your friend than I did as your lover, and that's been nice."

It had been.

"Rose played me for a fool and took me for one hell of a ride. But that's not on me. I'm a good man. I'm a good lover. I'm a good husband. I refuse to let her coldness break me." He shook his head. "Sure, I have trust issues, but my confidence has never wavered. Neither should yours. Because I've had the luxury of having you—and you're perfect."

I looked away at his final comment, feeling warmth replace the pain that had gripped my chest a moment ago.

"Have you seen him since it ended?"

I shook my head. "After we signed the papers, we never saw each other again."

"So, the divorce wasn't messy?"

"He was the one with the money, but I didn't want any of it. He got to keep the apartment and everything else, which was fine with me, because I would have just burned it down anyway." Half of his assets belonged to me, but I didn't want his wealth to be vindictive or greedy. I just wanted to start over, to make it on my own without looking back.

He stared at me with his fingers over his lips, his eyes dark.

"And I did."

He nodded. "Yeah...you did."

I didn't want to talk about my ex anymore. We were at a beautiful home with an incredible view, so he shouldn't be getting free rent through our conversation. "What kind of student were you?"

"Meaning?"

"Were you bright, or did you goof off all the time?"

He grinned. "Both."

"Really?"

He nodded. "I inherited my father's and grandfather's brilliance, but I was also a little shit who liked to stick my hand up the girls' dresses and steal my dad's car in the middle of the night."

"I can't picture you acting that way."

"I mellowed out in college."

"Except for the hand up the dresses part."

He chuckled. "That's only gotten worse as I've aged."

"What about your mother?"

"I won't sugarcoat it—she was a trophy wife. My dad was a rich guy who wanted a beautiful wife. But he definitely loved her. After she was gone, he never remarried or even tried to date. He always said she was his one and only."

"That's sweet…"

"Yeah."

"She never did anything at the company?"

"No. Stay-at-home wife. Did yoga every day. That kind of thing."

"Sounds nice."

"I never heard her complain." He drank from his glass and looked across the yard, his knuckles under his jaw.

"Why didn't your sister take over the company?"

"I'm older than she is, and when my father passed away, it just made the most sense at the time."

"But does she have greater ambitions?"

"I think so. She's the head of distribution, so she has a big job. But stepping up to my position… I'm not sure if she would ever want the job."

"Why?"

"She wants a family, and now that she's got a serious guy in her life, it might happen sooner rather than later."

"Women can have a family and run a company."

"I know, but I'm not sure she wants to do both. She knows how many hours I put in at home and on the weekends, so it makes my job much less desirable."

"What about two CEOs?"

He considered the question.

"You split the work, so you both have more time."

"Not a bad idea. But I'm sure she knows that's an option and has never pursued it."

"What do you mean, you're sure she knows?"

He turned back to me. "I've never assumed the role because I'm the oldest or because I'm a man. I've always told her, if she ever wants the job, I'll step down. The company belongs to both of us, not just me."

God, could he be any hotter? He was so confident that he wasn't intimidated by any event or any person. He had an open mind, not the least bit misogynistic. He didn't think less of me for my affair with the mafia, didn't care that I was so devoted to my job, which could be dangerous at times. He accepted me...exactly as I was.

"So, did your ex have a problem with your profession?"

"His name is Evan." If he was going to keep coming up, might as well just use his name. "And yes, sometimes."

"I read an article the other day that said the United States was one of the most dangerous countries for journalists. That three hundred of them had been killed doing their jobs just last year alone." He dropped his hand from his jaw and stared at me, gauging my reaction to the fact that he'd just spat out at me.

"Yeah, that's totally true," I said simply. "We've had a few people pass away in my office."

His eyes narrowed slightly, like that gave his heart a little jolt. "And you think you won't be one of them?"

"No. I just don't care if I am."

He stilled even more, as if he couldn't believe what I'd just said.

"My work is more important than my life. It's bigger than me. I understood that the moment I started. People enlist in the armed forces, knowing there's a chance they won't come back. People run into fires to save other people's lives even though they may lose theirs in the process. My job isn't that heroic, but the truth is worth the risk."

"But the statistical likelihood of something happening to you is much higher than either of those scenarios since there are far fewer journalists than soldiers and firefighters. And based on what I saw in the alleyway, you've had a lot of close calls."

"I wouldn't call them close calls."

He didn't express his anger, but his eyes showed it clearly. He was never easy to read, but right now, the words appeared on the page. He never showed his dislike for my job, but right now, he wasn't a fan.

"I've taken so many self-defense classes, martial arts classes, I have a gun—"

"You have a gun?" he asked in surprise.

"And I know how to use it."

He released a quiet sigh.

"I don't like where this conversation is going, Dax."

"Me neither." He looked away. "I care about you, Carson. I'd be devastated if something happened to you." He grabbed his water and drank the rest of it, wiping his mouth on the back of his forearm before he looked at the ocean.

My heart ached at his words. "If it ever does, just know I wouldn't have changed anything."

He closed his eyes for a moment, like that statement only made it worse. "Want to get some lunch? I'm starving." He rose out of the chair and grabbed the glasses before he carried them back inside.

"Yeah...sure."

SEVEN
DAX

Loud music played in the club, people dancing on the floor, bouncers hovering around the edges to make sure no one got out of hand. It was a new club in Manhattan and one that Clint had invested in.

I drank from my glass and looked across the room, staring at nothing in particular. The music was a cacophony to my ears, and despite the chaos of the noise and the crowd, it felt oddly quiet…because my thoughts were somewhere else.

Clint had his arm over the back of the couch, talking to a pretty brunette in a silver dress. Franco and Javier were doing much of the same, doing shots off tits and licking their lips. This lifestyle had been fulfilling in my twenties, but in my thirties, it started to feel stale. Every new club was like the one we'd been to before. Every woman in my bed was like the one I'd fucked the previous weekend. Every glass of scotch hit me less and less, because my tolerance had escalated over the past year.

Clint left his girl and fell into the empty spot beside me. "You're a billionaire in the hottest club in Manhattan, and you look like the saddest motherfucker on the planet. What the fuck, Dax?"

"I'm not sad."

"Mad?"

"No."

"Then what?"

The answer was obvious. "Bored."

He stared at me blankly for nearly a full minute. "You're *bored*?"

I nodded.

He looked around then came back to me. "Then there's something wrong with you because there's plenty of liquor behind the bar, beautiful women to fuck… What the hell do you want?"

"I don't know, man."

"If you're bored now, then you're going to be *really* bored at your birthday party on Saturday."

"Let me guess. Strip club?"

"*Private* strip club."

Yes, that did sound boring.

Clint continued to study my face. "Talk to me."

I shrugged.

"Let's have some pussy girl talk because that's obviously what you need." He grabbed his drink.

"What about your girl?"

"She'll wait." He pointed between our eyes. "Let's do this shit. Come on."

"I'm just stressed out."

"Something happen at Clydesdale?" he asked, his eyes turning serious when he thought my company was in jeopardy.

"No. Remember that woman I told you about?"

"You're still on her?"

"Well, we're friends."

"But you broke up like an eternity ago. Why is she still on your mind?"

I wished she weren't. "She's doing an article about me, so we've been spending time together."

"And?"

"I read an article that showed just how dangerous her profession is, and since she's so fearless as it is, I'm afraid something will happen to her."

"How is that your problem?"

I turned to him, my eyebrow raised. "Because I care about her...a lot."

"Then tell her to get a different job."

I shook my head. "Can't."

"Why?"

"I have no right to say that to her. And even if I did, she never would."

"Then get over her."

"I've tried."

"Bullshit, you've tried. You're spending all this time with her."

"We're friends."

"Okay, but fucking someone would probably help. You've been celibate a long-ass time."

Carson would never take me back, so I did need to move on. I hadn't actually tried. If anything, I only became more invested in that woman. Being her friend gave me what I'd wanted when we were dating, this raw openness that allowed me to see past her beautiful exterior and to the catacombs of depth beneath.

He looked across the club, and his eyes settled on a target. "Look at that bombshell in the blue dress. Go fuck her." He patted me on the shoulder.

"She's not a dog in heat."

"When she gets a look at you, she will be."

She was a beautiful woman with long brown hair, long legs, and full lips—exactly my type. My sex life had been stale for almost a month, and I was anxious to get laid, even though my mind wanted other things. But I knew Carson was hooking up with guys, even if she didn't say anything. That was what she did.

"Go, asshole. And don't come back." He pushed me out of the chair.

I straightened my jacket and shot him a glare. "Fine, I'm going."

"Good. Fuck her brains out."

I WALKED into the room at the gym with the basketball court. Charlie was already there with Matt, drinking from their water bottles.

Carson was nowhere in sight.

"Hey, man." I fist-bumped them both. "Where's Carson?"

"At work. She's coming straight here from the office."

I took a seat beside Charlie, wondering if Carson had told him about Denise. I didn't ask because I didn't want to spill the beans if he didn't know anything. Definitely not my place to share that information.

"She told me your place is a major fuck pad."

I was about to drink from my water, but I laughed instead. "What?" That sounded exactly like something she would say.

"I guess your folks' place is super nice or something," Charlie said.

She should see my place in the Hamptons.

"Yeah, but it's not really a fuck pad." My penthouse was closer to that description. "It's where I grew up, so there wasn't a lot of fucking going on, at least not from me." I'd moved out when I left for college, and my sex life hadn't been incredible at the time. Maybe my parents got it on, but I didn't.

"What are you going to do with the place?" Charlie asked.

"Why?" I teased. "You want to bring a date there."

"I mean…I wouldn't say no to that."

William walked inside, in gym shorts and a t-shirt. His towel was over his shoulder.

I raised my hand. "Over here."

William spotted me and walked over. "So, this is the crew, huh?" He took a seat and shook my hand.

"Charlie, this is my friend William," I said. "He's gonna play with us today."

"What's up?" Charlie shook his head. "This is my friend, Matt."

"Hey." Matt waved from his spot on the other side of Charlie.

"Glad you could make it," I said.

"I'm excited. But this isn't a scenario where I have to let you win, right?"

"No," I said with a chuckle.

"Good. Because I'm not gonna throw a game for anyone."

We left our stuff behind and warmed up on the court since we were waiting for Carson. She almost never took the bench because she was one of the best players. I introduced William to the rest of the guys, and we passed the ball around.

Carson walked in a moment later, in little shorts and a t-shirt. Her long legs were incredible, like always. Her hair was slicked back in that sexy ponytail that bobbed up and down when she ran across the court. With those beautiful green eyes and full lips, she was stunning, like always.

Fuck.

I walked over to greet her, wearing a smile I didn't feel in my soul. "What took you so long?"

"I work for a living, asshole." She gave me a gentle shove in my chest. "And if you're important, people will wait."

"You're definitely important."

"Because I'm the best player on my team." She placed her hands on her hips as she came closer. "Who's the new guy?"

"That's my sister's boyfriend."

"Ooh..." She looked him up and down. "Good-looking, decent shot, tall..."

"Important qualities?"

"Yeah. If this guy might be the father of your nieces and nephews, you want him to be all those things."

Never crossed my mind, but I was amused by her observations. "Including the decent shot?"

"Yeah. You don't want those kids to be picked last in gym, right?" She caught the ball Charlie passed to her while barely looking at him. She dribbled the ball and backed up a bit before she lined herself up and made a shot from the half-court line.

William turned to her, an eyebrow raised. "Damn..."

She smiled and extended her hand. "Carson. I'm friends with Dax."

He nodded. "Nice to meet you. I'd like to be on your team."

I held up my arms. "What the hell, man?"

He turned to Dax. "I told you I wasn't going to let you win." He caught the ball then dribbled to the hoop.

Carson came back to me, her hands on her hips. She was short in her running shoes, so she always had to tilt her head back to look up at me. "I like this guy."

I smiled as I looked into her face, loving her attitude, her playfulness. She was like one of the guys, but one of the sexiest chicks in the world. It was impossible not to fall under her spell...over and over.

AFTER THE GAME WAS OVER, we wiped the sweat off at the bleachers and prepared to get something to eat. The group decided on pizza and wings again, so we left the gym and walked up the street.

Carson walked up ahead with Charlie and Matt, while William and I stayed back a little bit, giving me a great view of her perky ass en route.

"You're a pretty good ballplayer." William uncapped his bottle and took a drink. "Play in college or anything?"

"No." I shook my head. "Just high school and recreationally. But Carson played in college. She's a Harvard alumnus."

"Really?" he asked in surprise. "People who go to Harvard or Stanford usually make it obvious they went to Harvard or Stanford," he said with a chuckle. "So, she seems pretty cool."

"She is." Despite her intelligence and her success, she never bragged, not once. She seemed to hide it rather than flaunt it, just the way I did. "She's an investigative journalist for the *New York Press*."

"No way, man. That's sick."

"Yeah. She's writing an editorial piece about me, actually."

"Oh, is that how you met?"

"No...we were friends already." I didn't want to share my personal bullshit with him. Seemed pointless since Carson and I were never getting back together. "So, were you at the office today?"

"I'm there Monday through Friday," he said. "And most Saturdays."

"Your practice is open on the weekend?" I asked in surprise.

"No. I just have to do a bunch of paperwork, you know, the business side of things."

"So, you own this practice?"

"Yep."

I liked that he didn't brag about himself either. Information came out naturally in conversation, but he didn't throw his accomplishments in your face. "So, you have to handle two things at once, a medical practice and a business?"

"Yeah...totally sucks."

I chuckled. "You know, you could hire a bookkeeper to help you with that. Maybe an assistant or something."

"I don't know... I believe if you want something done right, you have to do it yourself. I just have a hard time trusting other people, especially when it comes to stuff so personal, like my finances. Besides, I don't want to have a close relationship with an inferior in that regard, especially considering Renee."

I cocked an eyebrow. "Why?"

He grinned, like he was remembering something humorous. "My baby gets soooo jealous."

"She does?" I asked in surprise. "I can't see her being that way."

"Like I said, she's crazy about me." He grinned, like he was the luckiest guy in the world. "She'd be livid if she knew I told you this story, but fuck it, I'm gonna say it anyway. So, I was out with my brother's wife because we were planning his surprise party. She was at the same restaurant and spotted us together. Caused a huge scene, slapped me a couple times, stormed out…and then my sister-in-law explained the whole thing."

"Geez, that doesn't soud like her at all."

He rubbed his cheek like he still remembered how the slap felt. "Yeah, but it was kind of hot. She kept saying she wanted to take it slow, even though I was totally hung up on her, and then she did that…so she showed her true colors."

"Then meeting your parents must have been awkward."

He chuckled. "Yeah, she was pretty nervous. But my family is cool. They thought it was funny."

"I'm learning about a whole new side of my sister through you."

"Yeah, she's a little crazy, but I like her that way."

I'd tease her about this later.

"So..." He nodded up ahead. "What's the story with you two?"

"Who are you talking about?"

"The woman whose ass you keep staring at."

Was I making it that obvious?

He grinned. "Come on, I'm a doctor. I'm kinda smart."

"There's nothing there."

"Really? Because you talk about her a lot, and you have a lot of chemistry on the court."

We had a lot of chemistry in every way imaginable.

"You're a good-looking, down-to-earth guy. Why wouldn't she want you? Go for it."

I stopped pretending I didn't feel that way. "We used to be together, but I fucked it up."

"Oh...sorry, man. I didn't know."

"It's okay. I said we could just be friends."

"You mind if I ask what happened?"

It was crazy that the two of us hit it off so quickly. I got along with pretty much anyone, but William felt like an old friend who'd just come back to town. "The short version—"

"No, no, no." He waved his finger. "I want the longer version."

"Alright. Well, we kinda had a fling for a while, but I wanted more. She wasn't ready because she was still pretty hurt from her divorce, so she wanted to keep it casual. I was still fucked up from my divorce, but that didn't stop me from wanting more of her. I kept pushing, but I was also lying to her every single day."

"About?"

"I didn't tell her who I really was, that I'm a billionaire and CEO of my family's company. I even had a fake apartment so she would think I was just like everyone else. When the newspaper wanted to do a story on me, I specifically asked for someone else on the staff, but they sent Carson instead. Before I got the chance to come clean, she found out…in the worst way imaginable."

"Yikes…that's quite a story. But I never would have suspected something bad happened between you two since you get along so well."

"We talked it out and moved on."

"If you're still into her, why don't you try to make it work?"

I shook my head. "She said it's not going to happen. Her husband cheated on her, and she can't tolerate a man lying to her… I get it."

He nodded and released a sigh. "Not really the same thing, but I understand. Relationships meant to last should be built on trust and honesty. I've been really transparent with Renee because I never want to lose her. So, I've told her everything about me, even stuff I'm not proud of."

"Like?"

"Well…"

"You don't have to tell me, man. I shouldn't have asked."

"No, I've got nothing to hide. My buddies and I went to Vegas for a bachelor party, and I slept with a hooker. Not my finest hour. But we were all going crazy and threw caution to the wind."

It was a little embarrassing but not totally egregious. "Were you seeing someone at the time?"

"No. But you know, it's still kinda gross. Women are really turned off by that."

"How did Renee feel about it?"

"She was disappointed, but like I said, she's obsessed with me, so she brushed it off pretty quickly. And I outright told her about it and put it on the table, so I think she appreciated my honesty."

"Yeah." Why hadn't I done that?

"So, you're just friends? Like forever?"

"That's the plan."

"What a shame. Because you wear your heart on your sleeve, man."

I sighed and kept my eyes forward, watching her hair move in the wind. "Yeah. Haven't felt this way about anyone except my ex-wife, but that was all a lie and manipulation, so this is real...and it's different."

He turned to me, eyeing me sympathetically. "Maybe you should try again? People get back together all the time."

"But Carson isn't like other people..."

"Maybe. But when enough time passes, it could be different. She obviously doesn't seem angry with you, so I would try again...at some point. That's my best advice."

"Thanks."

We entered the pizza parlor and sat at the same table as last time. Beers were ordered, and since Matt would die if he didn't eat, we ordered right away. I took the seat beside Carson, with William across from me.

He drank his beer and behaved like a long conversation about my unresolved feelings for her never happened.

"Did you grill him?" Carson asked me, still stunning even when her makeup was gone and her hair was a little greasy.

"Why would I grill him?"

"You know, because he's trying to be a member of your family." She deepened her voice and tried to speak like a character from the *Godfather*. "He wants to be part of this family…he needs to earn it."

Charlie rolled his eyes. "Oh my god, I hate it when she does the *Godfather* voice."

William smiled, like he thought it was amusing.

Everything she did was amusing. She wasn't afraid to be goofy or different. Other girls cared about being beautiful all the time, quiet and polite, well-liked. Carson didn't care what anyone thought of her.

"I'm not trying to be a member of the family," William said. "At least, not right this second. Someday, yes. But she moves at the pace of an iceberg…"

"I think she'll be different after our talk," I said.

"She's definitely been in a better mood," William said.

"What did you think of his basketball skills?" Carson asked.

"You're really going to ask me that right in front of him?" I asked incredulously.

"It's good for him to know where you stand," she said. "Keep him in line."

"Damn, she's tough." William drank from his beer. "I'm glad she's not my girlfriend's brother."

"She's an even worse roommate," Charlie said.

She swatted him playfully. "Am not. You would die if I moved out."

"No, I think I'd be okay," he said sarcastically.

"Oh, come on," she said. "You would be totally heartbroken. There'd be no groceries in the house, no beer... What would you do without beer?"

"Well, I wouldn't have dirty dishes in the sink and pieces of popcorn stuck between the cushions in the couch," he fired back.

I noticed they fought like siblings, so that cured the jealousy I'd had long ago. They didn't tease each other in a flirtatious way. Charlie genuinely hated and loved her the way I hated and loved my sister.

"Oh, whatever." She rolled her eyes and drank from her beer.

William glanced back and forth between them. "Are you guys brother and sister?"

"Psh," Carson snapped. "He wishes."

Charlie shook his hand. "Being roommates is the extent of our relation."

The fries and wings came out first, and Carson ate like one of the guys, getting her elbows on the table, but she also kept her mouth clean with a napkin, eating like a lady with an appetite that rivaled ours.

The two of us got along together so well that sometimes I wondered how she could keep this distance from me. It just felt right, like we belonged together. Once we became completely honest with each other, it was even better than it used to be. Was I the only one who felt that? Was I stuck in my head, in a different reality?

When I looked at William, he was staring at me while he ate a few fries. He didn't say anything because the intention behind his gaze was clear. He saw the way I stared at Carson.

I just wondered if she noticed the way I stared at her too.

EIGHT
CARSON

Charlie and I sat at the dining table together, both working on our laptops, drinking beer. We'd had dinner hours ago, and now it was late into the night, the brightness from the screen making my eyes tired.

My phone lit up with a text message.

Boy Toy #1: *Still seeing that guy?*

After I read the message, I went back to my article.

Charlie must have read it because he said, "The apartment has been quiet."

"You want to get a dog?" I asked excitedly.

He gave me a cold stare before he rolled his eyes. "I meant you haven't brought any dates back to the apartment."

I shrugged then turned back to my computer.

"And you haven't been seeing anyone, as far as I can tell."

"What's your point, Charlie?" I spun my earring in my lobe while I read over the last few sentences I'd written.

"That's a long dry spell for you, is all. What? Four, five weeks?"

I shifted my gaze back to him. "I appreciate you checking in on my coochie, but she's fine."

He propped his chin on his closed knuckles and stared at me. "It just makes me wonder if you should forgive Dax—"

"I've already forgiven him."

"Alright, then take him back."

"Are we seriously doing this?" I closed my laptop slightly, so it was easier to look at him.

"You obviously have no idea what you're doing, so I've got to step in."

"I'm perfectly fine, Charlie." I opened my laptop again.

"He's not going to be available forever, you know."

"Good for him."

"Carson." He raised his voice slightly, his tone turning hostile.

I turned back to him, frustrated. "He put you up to this?"

"No." His irritated eyes burned into mine. "He doesn't ask about you. Doesn't talk about you. I'm saying this based on my own feelings about the situation. You obviously still have a thing for him—"

"I'm attracted to him. I'm not gay, so it's impossible not to be."

He shook his head. "Bullshit, it's more than that. He's not like Evan, so you're denying yourself a great guy because of a mistake he made."

"It wasn't a mistake. It was intentional."

"Whatever. That was five weeks ago. You guys are both connecting on a deeper level. It's so obvious."

"Because we're friends. Friends connect."

He sighed loudly. "Carson, why haven't you been sleeping around?"

"Because I'm busy—"

"Try again."

"What? I am," I snapped. "I've got four articles, basketball, now I want to get a dog—"

"Stop it." He dropped his hand on the table. "It's because of Dax. If you were really over him, you'd be texting this guy back. You'd be picking up some stud at the bar. You're coming home alone every night, and I know you aren't sleeping elsewhere. Do whatever you want, Carson. It's your life. But another Dax isn't going to come around, and you're going to lose a great guy because you're being too stubborn. Just my two cents."

I didn't want to hear his words, didn't want the truth to hit me so hard in the face.

He stared at me, as if he expected me to say something.

I wanted to change the subject, and since I had to talk to him about this anyway, I used it to my advantage. "There's something I need to tell you. I've thought about it for a while now, and there's really no good way to go about it.

And since you're my best friend, you're the person I come to."

His posture immediately changed, his eyes narrowing. "What is it?"

"Denise and I got a drink the other night…and told me she kinda had a thing for you."

His reaction wasn't subtle. His eyes widened in shock, like he couldn't believe those words just came out of my mouth. His fingers dug into his hair, and he turned away, inhaling a deep breath like the news was so good he didn't know what to do with it. "When did this happen?"

"Like a week or so ago."

"And she…" He narrowed his eyes on my face. "I'm not stupid, Carson. I know what you're really doing."

"I'm not lying about Denise. That really happened."

"But you can't just shrug off what I said about Dax."

I dropped my gaze and felt touched that he still cared more about me than the thing he'd been obsessing over for months. His loyalty was unshakable, and he cared about me more than himself. He was a good friend, more like family.

"He is a fucking catch. Some other woman is gonna come along and sink her claws into him, and then it'll be too late."

"I'm sure plenty of women are sinking their claws into him."

"And that doesn't have to be the case. Give him another chance."

"Look, I've heard you." I raised my hand. "I will consider what you said."

"There's nothing to consider. Be with him."

"You don't know what it's like to get your heart demolished, Charlie. You have no room to tell me how to feel, how to brush it off."

He shook his head. "You're acting like he did something really terrible to you."

"I'm not talking about him."

His eyes softened.

"I gave Dax more of my heart than I realized, and it left me so vulnerable. I'm just not ready for that again. There's nothing I can do about it. I can't force myself to be ready..."

"He'll take it slow."

"Doesn't matter. I can't force this. It's not fair to him or me. Now, let's move on because we've got bigger fish to try."

"I'm not sure if I agree with that, but whatever." He closed his laptop and pushed it to the side. "So, what exactly happened with Denise?"

"She's attracted to you, basically."

He grew excited again. "And she told you that you could share this with me?"

"No..."

His eyebrows rose.

"I'm in such a tough position right now. I can't keep everyone's secrets. I can't be loyal to everyone. Shit is gonna hit the fan regardless of what I do, so I may as well just put everything on the table and let it happen."

"Then what should I do?"

"Honestly, I get the impression it's just physical for her right now. Because she said she would never act on her feelings because of Kat, so maybe a one-night stand would work, but then she would feel too guilty about it."

He closed his eyes and dragged his hands down his face. "Jesus..."

"You can't just go for her because Denise will turn you down. And you shouldn't go for her unless there's a chance it could be more than physical, because you're hurting Kat for no concrete reason."

"Then what the fuck do I do?"

I shrugged. "No fucking idea."

He looked at the table as he sighed. "I...I'm really frustrated with this Kat situation. It's been nine months since we broke up, and that shouldn't stop me from being with the woman I really want—"

"Don't be cruel. The way you feel about Denise...is the way Kat feels about you."

He closed his eyes like that pained him. "Fuck." I felt bad for betraying Kat, but I couldn't keep all these secrets anymore.

"So, it's not going that well with Jeremy?"

"It's still early in that relationship."

"So, what am I supposed to do?" he asked incredulously. "Never make a move on the one woman I want because the woman I don't want who still wants me will get hurt?"

"I...I don't know."

He rubbed the back of his neck. "You realize I can't do that, right? I can't just ignore the way I feel."

"I know. So, we need to come up with the best way to do this."

"Is there a best way?" he asked.

"I could talk to Kat...or you could talk to her."

He shook his head. "I'm not gonna take her out for coffee and tell her I want Denise."

"Okay, then I'll do it."

"Still...weird."

"You guys date in private, and she finds out?" I asked. "That would be worse."

"Yeah."

This was so shitty, and I would be the one to take the most heat. "I think I should talk to Kat. Tell her that both of you have told me you're into each other...and I'm going to pass that information on. But first, I wanted to give her a heads-up."

"I guess that's a good way to go about it."

"And if she has a hard time with it, I can talk her through it, prepare her...et cetera."

"What if she says she doesn't want you to tell us?" he asked.

"I'll make sure she doesn't stick with that decision. That might be her initial response because she'll be emotional, but she'll see reason at some point. She's not a selfish person, so she'll get there."

He nodded. "I appreciate your telling me. I know that must have been hard for you."

"You have no idea."

"And I appreciate that you're doing everything you can to make it work out for everyone."

"Yeah…"

"That's the way I feel about you, which is why I think you need to work it out with Dax. Because he's the best thing for you."

NINE
DAX

"Happy birthday, motherfucker." Clint clapped me on the back when we entered the club, one of the hottest strip clubs in the city. The cost to rent out a place like this had to be a million dollars just for the night, but Clint and the guys split the cost to give me the party of a lifetime.

Women danced on the poles, topless waitresses walked around, and a group of beautiful women immediately came to me and escorted me into a chair. A crown was put on my head, my favorite drink was served, and I felt like a king.

Clint and the guys took a seat. Clint reached into his jacket and pulled out a stack of twenties. "Fight for it." He threw the bills into the air, and they cascaded down onto the floor. Girls got on their hands and knees and picked up as much cash as they could.

He pulled out a cigar and lit it, watching them fight like animals. "This is the life, isn't it?"

I stared at him, watched the smoke rise from the cigar and reach the ceiling, watched the greed and surge of power in his eyes. The rest of the guys were thrilled, grabbing asses as they passed, wearing their suits that cost as much as a car. Loud music played, the girls remained on the stage, and the darkness swept over us all.

THE SUNLIGHT CAME through the window and hit me right in the face.

I didn't want to wake up, but the sun forced me to.

I opened my eyes and sat up, knowing the switch to the blinds was above the nightstand.

But I was boxed in on both sides.

A brunette on one side, a blonde on the other.

I pinched the bridge of my nose and sighed through the migraine before I leaned over one of the strippers I'd brought home last night and flicked the switch.

She groaned then turned over so I wouldn't be in her way.

I hit the switch then grabbed the glass of water there. I took a big drink but felt the headache pound anyway.

The shades hummed as they fell down over the windows, bringing the bedroom into darkness.

This headache wasn't going to go away, so I crawled over one of the girls and got to my feet. I fished my phone from my pocket and then walked down the hallway. The rest of the penthouse was bright because there were no shades for all the windows, so I squinted as I made my way to the pantry and found the pills.

I swallowed them dry before grabbing another glass of water.

I leaned against the counter and drank it, rubbing the sleep from my eyes, feeling the soreness in my body because of all the crazy shit that happened the night before. I cupped my face and sighed before dragging my hands to my chin and letting them fall.

I stood in my twenty-million-dollar penthouse in the morning light, two gorgeous women in my bed, and felt empty, like I didn't have anything at all. I had a lot to be grateful for, not a single reason to complain when my life was so much better than most, but somehow…it wasn't enough.

My phone vibrated in my sweatpants.

I fished it out and looked at the screen.

It was Carson. *Got plans tonight?*

The bitterness in my mouth amplified when I heard her voice in my head. I could hear her excitement, her playfulness, like she was standing right behind me. Flashbacks of the previous night came back to me, the two women I pleased at once. There was no reason to feel guilty, but I did anyway. Sex was supposed to help me move on, but it only made it clearer that I hadn't moved on at all. In fact, it was making it worse. Every time I was with another woman, I wanted it to be someone else. The physical intimacy couldn't override the emotional attachment I'd formed with another person. The heart beat the brain—every time. *No. Why?*

We're going out to dinner if you want to join.

I should say no. I was hungover, felt like shit. But I couldn't resist an opportunity to see her, to feel that peaceful calm any time I was in her presence. *I'll be there.*

AFTER A DAY of hydrating smoothies and a love affair with my bottle of pills, I finally felt better. The girls left when they woke up, leaving their numbers even though I would never call. I was back to my old ways, a Manhattan playboy.

I felt too old for this shit.

Instead of walking to the restaurant, my driver took me. There was no reason to hide my wealth anymore, and I wasn't in the mood to walk five blocks there and back. The car pulled up, and I got out before I headed inside.

They were sitting in a booth, their drinks on the table with an appetizer in the center. It was Charlie, Matt, and Carson. Carson had just dipped a cheese stick into the marinara before dropping it into her mouth.

I couldn't stop the smile from spreading across my face.

"That looks good."

Carson chewed quickly so she could talk, but she bit off more than she could chew.

Charlie was beside her and rolled his eyes. "She says hi."

Matt patted the seat next to him. "Hey, man."

I took a seat across from Carson, who was still chewing as quickly as possible.

Charlie watched her and slightly shook his head. "Why do you shove the whole thing into your mouth? Why don't you take a bite like a normal person?"

She smacked him as she continued to chew.

The waitress came over, and I ordered water.

"Water?" Matt asked. "That's it?"

"Just not in the mood today..." If I drank another drop of alcohol, I might die.

Matt grinned. "Oh, I got it...crazy night, huh?"

I shrugged. "A bit."

"It was your birthday, right?" Charlie asked.

I nodded. "Yep."

Carson finally finished with her bite. "Okay, hi. Sorry. That was bad timing."

"No, that was a bad bite." Charlie eyed her with his elbows on the table.

"And happy birthday," she said. "You make thirty-one look good."

I gave her a slight smile. "Thanks." I noticed the bread crumb in the corner of her mouth but didn't tell her about it, because I thought it was cute. She was in jean shorts and a purple top, her curled hair over one shoulder, revealing her lovely fair skin, her beautiful complexion. Her mascara and eyeliner were heavy, giving her a sultry look that was nearly irresistible. I barely noticed the guys because she was the most addictive thing I'd ever seen.

"So, what kind of wild night did you have last night?" Charlie asked.

I didn't lie. "Strip club."

Carson didn't give any reaction, like that knowledge didn't bother her in the least.

"Not a bad way to spend a birthday." Charlie gave a glance at Carson before grabbing a cheese stick.

"It was my friend's idea." I didn't want to make it seem like I was the dirty playboy Carson had assumed I was when we first met. "They pooled their money together and rented the place out."

"Damn," Matt said. "Those are good friends."

I shrugged. "I think it was more of an excuse to party."

"You don't look hungover," Charlie noted.

"I've had a couple smoothies and lots of pills..." I took a lot to get rid of the headache that had nearly incapacitated me. I couldn't remember all the details of last night and I could handle booze well, so I really must have reached my limit.

"Well, I'm glad you were able to join us." Carson took a drink, but she licked her lips, and that was when she caught the breadcrumb on her tongue. Her eyes were kind and open, like there was no jealousy or possessiveness on her part.

It was hard not to be disappointed, not to feel that emptiness inside me grow even more. How could she turn off those feelings so easily? Why did mine linger and hers disappear entirely?

The waitress came back over. "Ready to order?"

"Yep." Carson didn't look at her menu. "I'll do the double-stack burger."

I grabbed my menu and looked for something.

Charlie and Matt ordered, which turned the attention back onto me.

"Uh, I'll do the Caesar."

Carson looked offended. "You're getting a salad?"

I hadn't eaten anything all day, but I still had no appetite after all the scotch and cigars from the night before. "Had a big lunch."

"Well, we can split my burger," she said.

I grinned. "Like you would ever share your food with anyone."

She took a drink. "With you, I would."

I held her gaze a moment longer, felt that connection that spiraled all the way down to my soul. Just a single look from her was more exciting than a private striptease. It satisfied my body without even touching me. It gave me what I was missing, when I wasn't even sure what that was. "Well, thanks."

WE TALKED ABOUT BASKETBALL, sports, the article Carson was writing about me, and other inconsequential things. There was no talk of money or fancy cars. It was a real conversation with real friends. It was nice, relaxing. Even with my high school friends, it wasn't quite this casual, but there was always a subtle hint of distance from all of them. My wealth hadn't changed our friendship much, but it did...a little bit. But with these guys, it really meant nothing, and it was so much better than my drunken night in the strip club.

Dinner was finished, so the waitress brought the tab.

I fished out my wallet.

"Nope." Carson took the tab. "I don't think so, birthday boy." They put their debit cards in the folder so they could split it three ways.

"Don't need to do that." I was touched by the gesture anyway, because Carson really didn't care about my fat wallet at all. She treated me like a regular person.

"Too bad."

The waitress took the tab, but she came back a moment later with a small cake with lit candles.

I saw the writing on the surface. *Happy Birthday, Dax!* So, it wasn't a free dessert offered by the restaurant.

Then Carson started to sing. "Happy Birthday to you..." The guys joined in.

I smiled as I watched the waitress set the lit cake in front of me. It was embarrassing, to have people sing to me on my thirty-first birthday, but I smiled as I watched Carson as her eyes lit up in excitement because it made her feel good to do something for me.

"Happy birthday to you..." She had a nice voice, could probably be a singer if she wanted to. Then she clapped quickly, with the guys.

"I thought you said you weren't going to pull any stunts."

She shrugged. "Guess I changed my mind. Now, make a wish."

There were two candles on the cake, a three and a one. I stared at her for another moment before I took a deep breath and blew out the candles. Her request suddenly made me feel empty again, because the one thing I wanted was inaccessible to me. There was really not a single thing in the world I wanted more. Nothing.

The waitress took back the cake to slice it in the kitchen.

But my eyes remained on Carson's face, my heart suddenly aching in a way it never had before. This dinner was so casual, and I hadn't even known the three of them for long, but it felt like they'd always been in my life. It was crazy to me that I met this woman in a bar, by chance, and now she was so important to me.

I couldn't think clearly anymore. Rational thought was gone. I spoke my mind and didn't think twice about it. "Take me back."

She immediately stilled at my words, the excitement fading from her eyes.

Charlie flinched at what I'd said before his eyes darted to Carson's face to see her reaction.

Matt glanced back and forth between us.

I didn't care that they were there. I didn't care about anything anymore. I'd spent the night with two women who somehow made me feel alone...and there were three of us. I lived for the chance to see Carson, fell harder for her after every intimate conversation we had. I didn't want to go back to a strip club. I didn't want another one-night stand. There was only one woman I wanted to be with.

"I will never lie to you again, Carson. I promise."

She breathed hard as her eyes filled with emotional gentleness.

"I...I don't want to be friends. I want you, all of you, because we're great together."

Charlie and Matt were both boxed into the booth and they couldn't slip away, so they had to sit there and try to act like they didn't exist.

"Please," I whispered. "I don't want to be with anyone else."

She held her silence, her eyes slowly dropping.

"Sweetheart, come on..."

She kept her eyes down, holding her silence for minutes.

The tension was killing me. What the hell was she thinking? Did she really put this dinner together because she wanted to be friends?

"I'm sorry..." That was her only statement, no further explanation.

It was like being stabbed right in the fucking throat. I couldn't breathe.

Charlie gave her a subtle nudge in the side.

But she didn't change her answer. "I just want to be friends."

It was a million times more painful than the first time we broke up. My feelings for her had only become stronger, had evolved into something much deeper. It was torture to be around her and not touch her, not kiss her, not hold her. We hadn't really had a chance to be together, and it was a fucking travesty that we never would. "Well...I can't be friends with you." It hurt me to say it, to lose her altogether, but there was no other option.

Her eyes filled with pain, like I'd really hurt her.

"I just...can't." I sank back into the booth, breathing hard because this was worse than my divorce. It was the most emotional day of my life since my father passed away. "Every time I'm around you, I just fall for you harder. I can't be with other women because it makes me miserable that I'm not with you." It took all my strength to rise out of that booth and prepare to walk away forever, to never see her face again, hear her voice. But I had to do what was best for me because my heart couldn't take any more of her punches. I started to walk away, my eyes down so I wouldn't have to look at her again. "Thank you for the cake..."

TEN

CARSON

It took me a second to process what happened, the drastic turn the evening took. We'd swerved off the road, and it all happened so quickly that I couldn't believe we were pinned against a tree off the side of the road.

It was so traumatic my brain froze.

The waitress came over and placed four slices of cake in front of us.

But we were all quiet.

Charlie stared at me, his expression saying everything his mouth didn't.

Matt was normally talkative, but he was speechless too, like he didn't have a single thing to say. There was cake in front of him, but he ignored it, which was saying something for Matt.

Charlie sighed. "What the fuck are you doing?"

"Let's not do this—"

"We have to do this. Because you're being a goddamn idiot right now."

"I'm not ready—"

"Then tell him you need more time. But don't lose him altogether. He'll wait for you."

"I'm such a mess right now. I don't want to ask him to wait for something that may not even happen, you know?"

He dragged his hand down his face. "You really don't trust the guy?"

"It's not that—"

"So, you do trust him?"

"I didn't say that either. I just think neither one of us is ready—"

"It doesn't seem like he cares about that, Carson." Charlie stared me down. "He wants to try to make this work, in any way that he can. You've been spending time together as friends for a month now, and you've gotten to know him even better. I think there are no secrets at this point."

I knew he was going to scream at me until he got his way. "Look, I really like him. And I just...I'm scared."

"Well, you need to grow a pair and get over it," he snapped. "Because if you stay scared, you're going to lose this guy. No, you already lost him. He's gone now."

Hearing Dax say he didn't want to be friends at all hurt more than his lie. Knowing we would never run into each other at basketball or the bar or wherever...was devastating. Now, he really was gone. Permanently.

"Get your shit together, Carson. He's the best thing that's ever happened to you."

Matt grabbed his fork and started to pick at his cake. He didn't participate in the conversation.

"I've only been divorced for a year—"

"That's plenty of time. If you continue to live in the past, you'll never be happy. And the best revenge is being happy. So, live well—and you can't live well alone. You need to pull your head out of your ass, Carson. If you don't, I'll do it for you."

THE DAYS PASSED with strange stillness despite how busy I was. I was all over the place, working on my articles, staying late at the office, getting to bed at some ungodly hour, just to wake up at sunrise the next morning.

But most of my thoughts were filled with Dax.

I remembered the pain on his face, the sincerity in his eyes, the intensity of the moment as he threw his heart on the table and let it pulse right on the surface. My response was cold, but his declaration had been so unexpected there had been no time to react, to prepare.

I felt like shit.

I didn't know what to do.

I still had to finish his article and had more questions, so I called his office and made an appointment. He said he didn't want to be friends, so I had no idea how our next meeting would go.

Within fifteen minutes of making the appointment, I got an email.

From: Dax Frawley

Carson,

If you have any remaining questions pertaining to your article, you can send them here.

DAX FRAWLEY

CEO, Clydesdale Software

IT WAS like a punch to the gut, the way he cut me out of his life like a surgeon removing an organ. It was sterile and clean. It hurt...a lot. I didn't respond back because I would only type my questions and say nothing else.

I still had to interview his sister, but that shouldn't be a problem.

ELEVEN
DAX

I stepped into Renee's office. "I just talked to the developers, and we're completely scrapping our previous idea. We're meeting up again in a week to see what they come up with, and I'll do my own research. So, you need to talk to the manufacturers and put everything on hold."

Her office was the complete opposite of mine. She had a white desk with a beautiful rug underneath. There were always vases of flowers everywhere. The walls had images of the beautiful countryside, reminding her of our home in Connecticut. Instead of looking like a corporate office, it was an office you'd see in *Home and Garden*.

She looked up from her laptop then shut it. "Alright, I'll handle it." She was in white pants that were high on her waist with a blouse tucked in. Her hair was curled and pulled over one shoulder. "How'd it go with William last week?"

"He didn't tell you?"

"I want your version."

I sat in the armchair facing her desk. "Pretty decent player."

"That's it?" she asked, her eyebrow raised.

"He told me about the hooker in Vegas."

"He did?" she blurted. "What? I can't believe he told you that."

"The guy doesn't care what anyone thinks of him. I like that."

"But still…"

"And he told me about your little tantrum…"

The blood drained from her face, and she suddenly looked pale.

I grinned at her embarrassment. "Didn't know you were the jealous type."

"Oh my god, I'm going to kill him."

"I thought it was a cute story, actually."

"That was the most embarrassing night of my life."

"He seemed to enjoy it."

"Well, he's…different." She looked away, like the memory still got under her skin. "I'm glad you two are getting along."

"He's easy to get along with. I like that he doesn't brag to impress me. I just discover more information through our conversations."

"Like?"

"The fact that he owns his own practice. Impressive."

She chuckled. "He's one of the top five cardiologists in the city, but I'm sure he didn't mention it."

"See? That's what I'm talking about." I snapped my fingers. "If you're successful, it doesn't need to be broadcast. Constantly bragging means you're insecure. He's not insecure at all."

"No, he's definitely not." She rolled her eyes. "Anyway...I'm doing an interview with Carson tomorrow."

The second Carson was mentioned, my lungs deflated like punctured balloons. I put her out of my mind as much as possible, and when she'd tried to come in and finish off her questions, I'd intervened and told her we would only communicate via email from now on.

I never wanted to see her again.

Just couldn't do it.

My elbow rested on the arm, and my fingers stretched across my jawline as I regarded my sister.

"Not happy about that?"

"The interview doesn't bother me."

"Then why did you get so low all of a sudden?"

I normally wouldn't say anything, but Renee had asked for a deeper relationship with me, probably because she had been close to Mom and they talked about a lot of things. She'd turned to Dad for advice too. They were gone, and she needed me to step up. So, I told her the truth. "We aren't friends anymore."

"Oh... What happened?" She leaned forward, her elbows resting on the desk, her hands coming together.

"We got together for a dinner. I thought it was just casual, hanging out with her and her friends. But it was actually to celebrate my birthday, and she got me a cake and everything..."

"That sounds nice. What's the problem?" Her eyes were soft as she regarded me, like my romantic problems were important to her.

I rubbed my fingers across my cheek. "There's just something about those quiet moments with her that make me feel... I can't really describe it. The night before, I went out with the guys and we hit up a strip club and all this bullshit, and I just... It's not me anymore. And having that quiet moment, just us in that booth, her sitting across from me... made me lose it. I told her I wanted to be with her, that I wanted her to take me back."

Her eyes widened. "You said that in front of her friends?"

"Like I said, I just snapped."

"Then what happened?" Her voice trailed off like she already knew the outcome.

"She said no." I'd relived that moment so many times, the way she rejected me, turned me down like her answer was so concrete that no amount of closeness would ever change our relationship. I'd never felt this way about anyone, not even my ex-wife, and I refused to believe Carson didn't feel the same. But she still didn't want me, even if her feelings lingered.

She shook her head slightly. "I'm so sorry."

"Yeah."

"And she doesn't want anything to do with you?"

"No. I was the one who walked away."

Her eyebrows rose.

"As friends, she was a lot more open with me and I got to know her on a whole new level, and it's just making it more difficult. I'm never going to move on if I see her all the time. I'm never going to give other women a chance if I'm sprung on some woman who doesn't want me."

Renee turned quiet and just stared.

I rubbed the scruff on my jawline then looked at her. "What?"

"I just... I didn't know you felt that strongly about her."

I shrugged. "Doesn't matter."

"I think it does matter."

"It's complicated. I wasn't interested in anything meaningful when I met her, and she wasn't either. So, our timing is terrible..."

"If you guys are in the same place, then it sounds perfect to me."

It had sounded perfect to me too. We could both grow together, both move on together, both find happiness in each other. "She doesn't see it that way."

TWELVE
CARSON

Renee Frawley was on a different floor, so there wasn't much of a chance I would run into Dax. He was probably aware of the appointment and would make sure we didn't cross paths.

I checked in with her assistant and was ushered in a moment later.

Renee's office couldn't be more different from his. It was like a spring day in the park—but inside a skyscraper with a view of more skyscrapers behind her. Vases of flowers were placed throughout the large room, and big, vibrant paintings of hydrangeas next to sea cottages hung above a white desk with a padded white chair.

Renee rose from her chair and greeted me with a handshake —but not a smile. "Take a seat."

When I was up close, I could see the subtle similarities she shared with Dax, but she had her own look. She was beautiful, just like in the pictures at the house. But many years had passed since those photographs had been taken, and she'd really turned into a stunning woman. "Thanks for meeting me today. I've gotten a lot of information already, but I just wanted to get an understanding—"

"Just ask your questions." She returned to her chair and stared me down, her laptop open in front of her, a cold frown on her face. It seemed like this was the last thing she wanted to do with her time. Dax was so down-to-earth, but she was nothing like him. She was colder than ice.

My instinct was to talk back, but since I needed something from her, I just ignored it. I opened my notebook and got straight to the questions. "Dax said joining him in the CEO position was always a possibility, but you probably wouldn't want it. Do you think that could change? And how do you feel about having a brother who so easily shares power?"

Her stare was just as cold as her voice. "How do I feel about having a brother who's the best man that I know?" She cocked her head slightly, as if I'd said something offensive. "Dax is an equalist who has always treated me like I have just as much right to this company as he does. There's not a misogynistic bone in his body, because our parents were exactly the same way. Dax would do anything for me within a second, and if it were my wish to be the single CEO of this company, he would vacate the chair immediately. He's not some egotistical, greedy asshole who only cares about his bank account. He is, undoubtedly, the most wonderful man on this planet. That's how I feel about it, Carson."

Jesus Christ, that hostility was like an inferno. "We've gotten off on the wrong foot, and I have no idea why. Did I do something to offend you?" Instead of apologizing right away to kiss her ass, I didn't. I didn't apologize unless I meant it, and I didn't bend to anyone just because they were richer than I was. I came here as a professional, but she'd been pissed off since she laid eyes on me. William was kind and easygoing, so I found it hard to believe this was her usual character.

Her eyes narrowed farther. "I don't like you."

"Whoa...just gonna come out and say it, huh?" I gave a slight shrug. "Well, I have to commend you for your honesty."

She was still, her arms on the sides of the chair, regarding me like a ruler.

"I'll just stick with the questions then and disappear as quickly as possible." I didn't ask her why she felt that way because it really didn't matter. I hadn't done anything to deserve this disrespect, so I wouldn't humor her by pretending to care whatever her ridiculous reason was. "The company has been in the family for three generations, which is quite an accomplishment—"

"I don't like you because of the way you treat my brother."

I'd thought it was a possibility she wouldn't like me because of my personal relationship with her brother, but I didn't think she would lose all professionalism over it. "You mean, the way I was upset when he lied about who he was entirely? Took me to a fake apartment so he could be something he wasn't?"

Her anger increased. "He's a good man, Carson. I'm not saying that as his sister. He's not like the friends he hangs out with. He's honorable and, despite his mistake, honest. And the way he feels about you...is real. I don't appreciate the way you're holding a grudge against a man who obviously would do anything for you."

I bowed my head. "No offense, but it's complicated—"

"It's not complicated at all." She lowered her voice, which somehow made her more sinister. "My brother feels very strongly about you, has heartbreak in his eyes, and you're an idiot for continuing to play with his heart."

"I'm not playing with his heart—"

"Get your shit together and give him a chance. Because I promise you, you will never find a better man. You will lose your shot and regret it for the rest of your life. I'm sorry you've been hurt, and I understand new relationships are terrifying, but his lie was harmless. Stop being stubborn. Stop being difficult."

The last thing I'd expected was to have a conversation about my relationship with her brother, especially at this intensity. "If you don't like me, why would you even want me to be with him? He can find someone much better than me."

"Because you're the one he wants. Make him happy, then we have no problem. Make him unhappy…I'm your biggest enemy."

CHARLIE GLARED at me the second I walked in the door.

"Okay, this shit is getting old." I dropped my bag on the table.

"It's not going to stop." He sat in front of his computer in his sweatpants and a t-shirt. "Your head is still in your ass."

"Seriously, I'm not in the mood right now." I sat down and pulled out my phone. I started firing off texts, getting the girls to go out for a drink. The week had been rough, and I wanted to forget about all the drama.

"What's up?"

"I interviewed Dax's sister…"

"And that didn't go well?"

"She drilled into me harder than you did."

He cocked an eyebrow. "Meaning?"

"She basically told me off for hurting Dax."

"Good. I hope that lit a fire under your ass."

"I can't believe he told her about us. Do people really share that stuff with their sister?"

"You tell Denise stuff."

"But we're both girls."

He shrugged. "They're orphans."

Dax had told me they'd gotten closer. Maybe he was opening up to her more, which included details about me.

"You know, you could make this *all* go away if you just talked to Dax."

"Wow, that's really romantic," I said sarcastically. "I'll tell him the only reason I've come back is because everyone in my life hates me…"

He sighed and relaxed against the chair. "You honestly don't want him back? That's my issue. I know you do, but you're stubborn. If you just didn't want him, I'd let it go."

I pulled out my laptop and opened it on the table. "Can I just have some space with this?" It was my life, not his. It was my relationship, not his. "How am I supposed to think when I have people harassing me everywhere I go?"

He raised both hands in the air. "Fine."

I got responses from the girls. "We're going out tonight. You guys can join if you want."

"We?" he asked, his interest piqued.

"Yes. Me, Denise, and Kat."

He wasn't going to say no to that. "I'm in. I'll let Matt know." He pulled out his phone and sent the text. "When are you going to talk to Kat?"

I sighed. "I don't know, Charlie. I've had the week from hell..."

His eyes softened. "Yeah, I get it."

"I'll feel her out tonight and then go from there."

"Okay."

I did a few things on my laptop before I closed it and stood up. "I need to start getting ready."

"Who are you trying to impress?"

I rolled my eyes. "I don't get ready to impress a guy. I do it for myself."

―

OF COURSE, Dax was the topic of discussion.

"Just take him back," Denise said. "Come on, you guys have insane chemistry."

"And he didn't do anything *that* bad," Kat said. "I get why you were mad for a while, but it's been over a month and you guys are great together."

"Girls." I raised my hand. "The last thing I want to talk about is him, so let's just discuss something else."

The girls exchanged a look before sipping their drinks.

Charlie and Matt came to the table with their drinks. Charlie's gaze immediately went to Denise before he abruptly looked away, like he was really trying not to make his feelings obvious in front of Kat.

"How are things with Nathan?" I asked.

"Good." She took another drink. "We went to that new Chinese place on Seventh the other night. We're getting along pretty well."

"So, fireworks and butterflies?" I asked, hoping she was getting more detached from Charlie.

"I mean, there's definitely chemistry." Kat wasn't as forthcoming as usual, probably because Charlie was standing there, which didn't bode well for us.

"Still seeing that doctor?" Kat asked Denise.

"Oh no," Denise said quickly. "He'd asked me out a couple times, and I just caved. He's nice and everything, but it just wasn't right." She turned to Charlie. "What about you?"

Charlie looked like a deer in headlights. "I'm not seeing anyone, like, at all."

I glared at him.

He drank from his beer and looked away.

Matt glanced past us. "Looks like Nathan and Dax are here."

"They are?" Kat turned around to check.

My heart dropped into my stomach. I'd decided to go out to stop thinking about my situation with Dax, but instead, we were in the same place. We hadn't spoken in person since that horrible birthday dinner. He said he didn't want to be friends, but there was no way for us to never cross paths again since some of our friends were dating.

"Oh yeah," Kat said.

I didn't look.

Denise turned to me. "Are you going to climb out the bathroom window?"

I rolled my eyes. "If I want to leave, I'll` just strut out. I don't care. But no, I'm not a coward."

"Ooh, Jeremy is here too." Matt wiped his lips to make sure nothing was on his face.

There were a million bars, and we had to meet at the same one?

"I'm gonna go say hi." Kat walked away.

Charlie shifted his gaze to me as he drank from his beer.

Denise stared at me too.

"What?" I asked, offended.

"How are you going to handle this?" Charlie asked.

I shrugged. "It's his call, really. He's the one who said he wanted nothing to do with me."

After talking for a while, Dax and his crew came to join us.

Ugh.

Jeremy and Matt paired off, their arms around each other as they stood close together. Kat moved in near Nathan, either because she was genuinely happy to see him or she was trying to make Charlie jealous, which was pointless.

Dax joined the table—and acted like I didn't exist.

He stood beside Charlie, and they talked like nothing had happened, like they were still the best of friends.

Denise kept glancing at me. "So, tell me about that article you're working on."

I knew she was trying to keep me distracted; that way, I wouldn't focus on the man who wouldn't even look at me. "I've been writing about..." I blabbed on, but my eyes kept shifting back to him. He had one arm on the table with his fingers wrapped around his beer, and he was in a black tee that made his frame look incredible...like always. His jawline was sprinkled with masculine scruff, and his eyes were bright with excitement, like he really enjoyed his conversation with Charlie...my best friend. And he wore a handsome smile like he didn't have a care in the world.

Like this wasn't painful at all.

"Ugh. Oh my god." Denise's entire composure changed, her drink moving to the table, her eyes unblinking. Her tone was different from usual, like something truly alarmed her.

"Girl, what is it?"

She stared across the bar at something, looking past Dax. "Oh fuck... It's him."

"Who?"

She turned back to me, looking too distressed to give an answer.

I looked to where she was staring.

Kat must have noticed him too because she ditched Nathan and came closer to me. "Carson, Evan is here."

I didn't need her to tell me that…because I saw him.

He was with his friends, people who used to be part of my life, people who used to play board games in the living room. They were people whose names had always been in my message box. But then they disappeared once the divorce happened.

I hadn't seen Evan since I'd picked up my shit and left. We divided our things and never spoke again. It was a clean break. It was a big city, and I stopped going to all the spots we enjoyed to make sure we never bumped into each other. I got a new grocery store, gym, dentist, everything.

To make sure this moment never happened.

Now, I couldn't stop staring…because he was wearing a wedding ring.

"That motherfucker." Denise grabbed her drink. "I'm gonna throw this shit in his face."

"Whoa, hold on." I grabbed her wrist and brought her back. "You aren't doing anything."

The commotion brought the attention of everyone else at the table—including Dax.

Charlie looked over his shoulder, spotted Evan, and turned back to me. "Shit."

God, this was a nightmare.

"He's coming this way," Kat said. "Quick, kiss a hot guy or something."

"What?" I asked incredulously.

"He's already married?" Charlie asked. He shook his head, clenched his jaw, and made a fist on the table. "Fucking piece of shit."

"Best revenge is to show him how much better off you are than he is," Kat said. "Jackass is married, so you need to make out with someone or something. Use Nathan."

Nathan immediately looked uncomfortable.

"Okay, let's just chill out..." I wasn't going to make out with anyone.

"Then find a hot guy," Denise said. "You can walk up to any guy you want, and he won't mind."

"Dude, he's coming, and he's totally going to see you," Kat said. "Use Charlie."

Charlie didn't grimace because he was too pissed off. "How about I just punch him in the face instead?"

I covered my face with my hands. "Everyone, calm the fuck down. I don't need to make out with anyone." I dropped my hands and saw him come closer with his crew, smiling and having a good time like I was the last thing on his mind...and he hadn't thought of me once since I left. He would definitely see me, and I didn't know what to do. It seemed cowardly to pretend not to see him, but I didn't know what kind of reaction to give? Should I smile like I was totally fine? Should I glare at him because he was a piece of shit? I didn't know. We were together for years, so he would read my reactions well, see the pain in my eyes...and would know I was still a wreck while he'd clearly moved on.

Dax moved around Charlie and came toward me, looking right into my face for the first time since he'd come over here. His movements were slow and he didn't rush, but the intention in his gaze told me exactly what he was going to do.

Everyone stilled and watched us.

I was frozen to the spot, my heart pounding so damn hard.

He moved into me effortlessly, one hand sliding into my hair with a sexy tug, his other arm curving around my waist and pulling me hard against his chest. His lips dropped onto mine with a gentle landing, our mouths coming together like two pieces of a puzzle.

I forgot about Evan.

I forgot what I was doing.

One of my arms circled his neck, while the other rested on his arm, my fingers digging into his bicep through his sleeve. My mouth parted automatically to let him have me, to let that exquisite kiss light my entire body on fire and make my writhe.

It was such a good kiss, just like it used to be, with all the passion and desire that used to make my toes curl.

His fingers moved deeper into my hair, and the kiss became more intense, his lips taking charge of my mouth, sucking my bottom lip before giving me a flawlessly executed swipe of his tongue.

I brought him closer and let our mouths move together perfectly, the loud music suddenly quiet, the conversations nonexistent. It was just the two of us, a man and a woman caught in the deepest embrace.

I forgot my ex-husband entirely.

His arms hugged me hard, one hand moving to my ass like old times. If this was all show, he deserved an Academy Award. But I knew it was real, that he wanted to kiss me, wanted any excuse to have me.

And I wanted him to take as much as he wanted.

Once his lips were on mine, there was no reservation. It felt right, like this was the man who should have been my husband, not the jackass who had already moved on to wife number two. The kiss had gone on long enough, but we didn't pull away. It continued like no one was there at all...except us.

DAX DIDN'T SAY a word to anyone there. He ended the kiss and took me by the hand, guiding me out of the bar. He led the way, his height and size parting a path through the crowd so we could make it outside.

I didn't resist and didn't ask any questions. Not only did I forget about Evan, but I forgot about my friends too, didn't even think to look at their reactions to what just happened.

He took me outside and guided me to the curb where a blacked-out car sat. He got me in the back seat then joined me on the other side.

The driver pulled away, and he seemed to know where to go without instruction.

I turned to Dax, seeing the way the lights from the city moved over his face as he stared out the window.

He didn't look at me.

I looked forward again, my heart still racing. He was either driving me to my place or his, but I didn't know which one. I didn't dare ask, because he seemed angry based on the energy that radiated from his exterior.

The driver eventually pulled up to my building.

How did the driver know where to go?

Dax got out but didn't take my hand this time. We made the entire walk in silence.

When we got to the apartment door, I unlocked it, never so nervous in my life. I'd been to many places, done a lot of dangerous things, but this was terrifying. I walked inside, my heels tapping against the hardwood floor. I dropped my clutch on the entryway table then turned to him.

He stared me down, his height not towering over me because I was in a ridiculous pair of heels. His mouth was nearly level with mine, his eyes too. All he had to do was drop his chin a little bit and he could burn me with his dark gaze.

I stayed quiet…speechless.

His arms remained by his sides, and he continued to stare, his eyes shifting back and forth slightly. "We are together." His voice was crisp, a sharp sound in a silent room. "Just you. Just me. No friendship. I'm your man. You're my woman. Period. Do you understand me?"

I didn't respond to orders well, but his authority rendered me silent.

"I asked you a question, sweetheart." The affectionate nickname didn't dim his aggression.

"Okay…"

He stared at me for a while, as if he was surprised by my agreement, as if he expected it to be harder than that. "We can do this however you want to. We can go as slow as you want. The details don't make a difference to me. But no more bullshit about us being friends, about not being ready to be with me. Because I'm not ready to be with you either, but I want to be with you, regardless. That's what a relationship is, working through the difficulties—together."

All I could do was breathe. It was rare for anyone to shut me up, but he could make me quiet with his kiss and his words.

He stared at me for another minute before he turned to leave.

I grabbed him by the forearm and yanked him back, my body moving into his, and we thudded as we collided together. My fingers moved into his hair, and I kissed him, pulling him close, my hand gliding across his chest.

He kissed me back with the same passion, his anger making the kiss harsh and sexy. His large hands squeezed me, his fingers dug into my hair, his mouth ate mine with heavy breaths. Then he abruptly released me and walked off, leaving the door wide open without looking back.

THIRTEEN
CARSON

I woke up the next morning to the smell of coffee since Charlie already had the drip going. In my sweatpants and a baggy shirt without a bra, I yawned as I walked past the living room to the kitchen.

Charlie was at the table, and he stared at me the second I walked inside.

I grabbed a mug and filled it with coffee, the aroma hitting me in the face with the steam. I took a sip then moved to the dining table, where my laptop remained since I'd left it there the night before.

Charlie continued his stare.

I drank my coffee and rubbed the sleep from my eyes.

He glanced at the hallway, like he expected someone else to join me. "Is Dax here?"

"No."

"Then what happened last night?"

"He dropped me off and went home." I yawned again.

He gave me a quizzical expression. "You better start elaborating. You guys had a make-out session worthy of the *Notebook* before it segues into a dirty porno."

"Yeah…it was pretty great, wasn't it?"

His eyes narrowed. "What does that mean? Are you back together or what?"

I shrugged.

"Okay, stop it."

"What? Am I annoying you?"

"A bit," he said sarcastically.

"He dropped me off and left. That's it."

"Come on, there's more than that."

"Well…he said we're together, and that's the end of the story."

He grinned. "Good."

"That was pretty much it."

"I'm surprised you didn't sleep together."

"He seemed pretty angry, so…"

"He didn't look it when he kissed you." He grabbed his mug and took a drink. "And by the way, Evan saw…and stared."

"Yeah?" Honestly, I didn't really care.

"Dude, he stared hard."

"Dude?"

"I'm just happy that we got back at him. I can't believe he's already remarried."

"I'm sure his wife is his assistant..." The woman he cheated on me with.

He studied me for a while, his fingers around the handle of his mug. "You doing okay?"

I shrugged. "I'm not going to lie and pretend it doesn't hurt...because it does. But I'm doing better than I thought I would be. It was weird to see Eric and Jason, people we used to see all the time. Eric and I planned Evan's birthday party all those years ago, and now they're strangers to me. Someone replaced me...like that."

"Don't let it get you down. It says more about them than it does you."

"I know."

"And if he cheated *with* her, he'll cheat on her."

"I hope not—no one should go through that."

He watched me. "Even though she slept with your husband, knowing he was your husband?"

I shrugged. "I wouldn't wish it on anybody."

He shook his head. "He never deserved you."

I drank my coffee and pulled my knees to my chest.

"What's next with Dax?"

"Not sure."

"You're going to give this relationship a try, right? No more walls. No more running."

"I guess."

"Come on, I want to hear more confidence than that."

"He told me we can do it however I want, so I guess that does give me some confidence. He won't try to force me to be more than what I'm ready for. It's kinda like a blank canvas."

He nodded. "That's right for you guys."

"Yeah." I drank from my coffee again.

"You don't seem thrilled."

I set my mug down. "It was just a crazy night, you know? And honestly, Dax and I didn't really talk at all. He kinda just ordered me around and left, so I know he's still mad at me. But when he kissed me…it made me realize it was right. It wasn't just the kiss itself, but the fact that he stepped in and made me forget about the man who forgot me so easily. He's been hurt, I've been hurt, and I know I could feel so much for him if I just let myself. Maybe it's time to let myself."

He pumped his fist in the air. "Hallelujah."

"I haven't been with anyone because he's the only man I want to be with, so…maybe I should be with him."

"Couldn't agree more. I love Dax. He's the man."

"You loved Evan too."

He rolled his eyes. "I was naïve then. He's always been a piece of shit, I just didn't see it. Now, Dax, on the other hand—real deal."

"We'll see."

HE DIDN'T TEXT me for days.

Didn't call.

Nothing.

So, on my way home from work, I called him.

He answered right away, but he answered with his silence.

"Hey." I walked down the street, my phone in my pocket because I had the earbuds in my ears.

There was a pause before he responded. "Hey."

"Haven't heard from you."

"I'm done chasing you." His tone was clipped, like he was still angry. "Waited for you to come to me this time."

I knew I deserved that, so I took the hit. "Well, here I am, chasing you."

He breathed a quiet sigh into the phone. "Come by my place."

"Right now?"

"Yes."

I'd only been there once, but I remembered the way. "Alright."

He hung up.

I walked to his building, checked in with the security officer, and then rode the elevator to his floor. The doors opened like last time, silently, and revealed the sleek penthouse ideal for a handsome playboy.

It was later in the day and the end of summer, so the sky was turning pink and orange from the approaching sunset. Some of his lights were on, and he sat on the couch in front of the TV in just his sweatpants and nothing else.

Every time I saw him, I realized I'd forgotten how hot he was.

I stepped inside, and the elevator closed behind me. It was the first time I'd been in this multimillion-dollar piece of real estate as more than just a friend. It changed the tone, changed the expectations.

He didn't rise to greet me. He leaned back into the couch and stared at me. A decanter of scotch was on the table, along with a full glass. One arm was over the back of the couch, and he stared at me with that cryptic stare. His look was almost hostile because it was so intense. It was the same way he looked at me the night we met, that silent and brooding expression. He was the strong and silent type once more. He went back and forth, easy to talk to like a friend and then the indecipherable, rugged man who spoke like a caveman.

I walked to the couch and took a seat beside him.

He turned his head my way, looking at me next to him. His arm touched the back of my neck.

I was in my work attire, a skirt and blouse, my satchel with me. I let it sit on the spot beside me on the couch. When I looked at him, I didn't know what to say. It was easy for me to navigate the most difficult situations, but with him, I didn't have a voice. No one ever left me speechless, and I knew it was because I was afraid.

Even though I wasn't afraid of anything.

His brown eyes were on mine, deep and captivating. They shifted slightly as they regarded me.

I knew he wasn't going to say anything, so I went first. "It was easy to get close to you as friends because you were no longer a threat. But now that it's off the table, I'm tense all over again. It's not that I don't want to be with you. I'm just afraid, afraid because the feelings you have...I have them too."

Once I started to be vulnerable, that tint of hostility began to fade from his gaze. "Good start."

"I want to take this slow."

"Okay."

"No pressure."

"Alright."

"And how we were friends before...I don't want to lose that. It allowed me to give myself to you in the way I do with Charlie and Kat."

His eyes softened. "That's the part of our relationship I enjoyed the most. I don't want to lose that either."

"Okay...good."

His hand moved off the couch, and his fingers slid into the back of my hair, playing with the soft strands, slowly massaging the back of my neck. "We can take this as slow as you want. I just want to be together...because you're the only woman I want to be with."

My lungs immediately drew breath.

"I won't lie to you ever again. I will be faithful to you. I will never hurt you."

"You should never say never…"

"Well, I can say it." His fingers stopped in my hair. "Because it's not easy for me to feel this way about someone. I didn't even feel this way about Rose. You're…different. I'm a loyal man, and when I commit to something, it's a hundred percent. I understand you're still in a fragile place, that your heart has never really healed since Evan, but you'll trust me fully eventually. You've just never tried before."

"I did try," I whispered. "I saw all the signs that you were lying, but I chose to ignore them…and trust you."

His fingers stilled as the guilt moved into his eyes.

"Don't rewrite history, Dax. I did try, and it was difficult. Stop making this seem like it's entirely my fault. The reason we're here is because you lied, so let's not forget that."

He dropped his hand from my hair and returned it to the couch. "Alright. But we need to stop living in the past. We have a completely different relationship now. I want a clean slate, a real chance. Can you do that or not?"

I didn't want to run away from this man anymore, not when my heart was in his palm. I gave a nod.

"Okay." His hand moved back into my hair. "When we were apart, I was with other women…just so you know."

I'd already assumed that was the case, but it didn't soften the blow. It hurt, made me sick, picturing him fucking someone the way he used to fuck me. I wasn't the jealous type, but I was immediately uncomfortable with the idea of the supermodels who'd replaced me.

He stared at me, as if he expected me to reciprocate.

"I...I wasn't with anyone."

He stilled at my response, as if he'd expected me to say there had been dozens of men in my bed the moment he was gone. He seemed genuinely surprised, like my celibacy hadn't been an option.

I was almost embarrassed that I hadn't moved on like I usually would, because it was a dead giveaway to how I really felt, that I was heartbroken the entire time we were apart, that I only numbed my heart but never turned it off. When I was out at restaurants and bars, the offers poured in. I flirted with a handsome guy in a suit who I met at the coffee shop, but when he gave me his number, I threw it away. There was only one man I wanted to be with, even though I wouldn't admit it to myself.

He continued to stare at me, like he had no idea what to say. "I only did it because I thought I couldn't get you back...and I thought it would help me move on. But it only made me feel worse, because every time I was with you, I knew it was what I really wanted. Clint rented out this strip club, and money was flying in the air, naked women were crawling all over us and the floor, and he turned to me and said we had the best lives... And it hit me so hard. That was the kind of man I used to be, an obnoxious playboy who has so much money that he throws it at strippers on a drunken night. But all I really wanted was to have a quiet night with you. I wanted to watch the game with your friends. I wanted to have a deep and meaningful relationship with one woman... and get out of that strip club as quickly as possible. Knowing I'd ruined it, that I'd let the past sabotage the greatest thing that ever happened to me, just made me drink more." He looked away, like the memory of that emptiness was too much to think about.

"It's okay…"

He turned back to me, the pain still in his eyes.

My hand moved to his chest, sliding over the hard surface until I could feel the racing beat of his heart.

He stared at me for a while before his fingers slid into my hair again. Then he pulled me closer, bringing my face to his so he could rest his forehead against mine. He didn't kiss me, just held me there, like all he wanted was our closeness. His fingers stroked under the fall of my hair, feeling my neck.

My palm glided farther over his chest and to his shoulder until my arm hooked around his neck. I came closer to him then rested my head on his shoulder, my skirt riding up as I curled my legs behind me on the couch.

His arm wrapped tighter around me, and he rested his lips against my forehead, holding me close like he wouldn't let me go. His skin was hot to my cheek, and he smelled like pure man. It was like getting in bed after a long day, despite his hardness. It was home, going back to your childhood house for the holidays. "You're the only man I want…"

FOURTEEN

DAX

I didn't care how slow she wanted to go.

I didn't care if she was the one behind the wheel or I was in the cockpit.

I just wanted to be on the journey—wherever we went.

Once I had her on the couch, everything felt good. My heart finally relaxed now that she was mine. I didn't have to settle for being her friend when I wanted to be the man in her bed every night. I wanted her to be the woman in mine. The last six weeks had been unbearable because being her friend only made me realize what I'd truly lost.

I didn't have that problem anymore.

Our relationship had been built on sex, meaningless, no-strings-attached kind of sex. It was fun at the time until I actually started to care for her. The dirty pictures she sent me were still on my phone, but I decided to delete them because it felt like a completely different woman to me now.

I wanted more than that.

She was welcome to send me more and I would cherish them, but the past…I wanted nothing to do with that.

We were different people now.

I wasn't sure if we would sleep together anytime soon, but I got tested to make sure I was clean when the moment did arrive. Since she hadn't been with anyone, I didn't need to see her papers if she had them.

I went to work like usual then went home. Instead of blowing up her phone, I tried to behave the way I had before…when we were friends. She asked to take it slow, and I wasn't entirely sure what that entailed, so I chose to play it safe.

When Wednesday night came around, I headed to the gym with the assumption she would show up with Charlie and Matt. I practiced a few shots on the court with the guys, one eye on the doorway, and when she walked in, I passed the ball and walked to the benches to meet her.

She was in her little shorts and top, a sexy, fit chick. When she wasn't in her sky-high heels, she was so small and petite, and she seemed to be more ferocious to make up for it. She set down her water bottle along with a towel then turned to me.

I looked into her face, feeling a rush of joy because this felt right. Those two strippers in my bed on the night of my birthday…did not feel right.

Then she smiled at me, the kind of smile that lit her eyes with radiant light.

I lived for that smile.

"You're going to take off your shirt for this game, right?"

Now, I smiled. "Gonna check me out, sweetheart?"

"It's literally the only reason I come every week." She moved into me, and like she'd done it a hundred times, rested one palm against my chest and rose on her tiptoes to give me a kiss.

I kept my hands on my hips and didn't grab her the way I wanted. I kept everything contained, restrained myself from kissing her the way I'd demolished her lips in that bar, the way I'd shown her ex what he was missing, not for Carson's sake, but because of my own possessiveness.

She pulled away then walked onto the court.

I gave her ass a playful smack.

She turned around and walked backward, waggling her eyebrows jokingly before she faced forward again and approached the guys. "Who's ready to kick some ass?"

I watched her go, seeing that fine piece of ass shake.

Charlie came to my side. "I'm happy for you, man."

I turned to him and shook his hand. "Thanks."

"And she's happy too." He nodded in her direction, her hands on her hips.

"That's what I want to hear."

"Just be patient with her. She didn't say much, but I know that whole thing with Evan really bothered her."

I hadn't actually considered it because I'd been thinking about myself, about getting the woman I wanted.

"I don't think she's sad that he's moved on, by any means. But...it's pretty cold that he is already remarried when it's been a relatively short amount of time. Just the fact that she never really meant anything to him...is a tough pill to swallow."

My eyes shifted back to her on the court, watching her play with the guys with a focused look on her face, treating the sport competitively like it was being televised. "Yeah..."

"Just giving you a heads-up about the whole thing. I *really* want this to work."

I gave a slight smile but didn't feel it this time. "I can tell."

He clapped me on the back then headed onto the court. "Good luck out there...even though we're gonna kick your ass."

CARSON WAS playful on the court. Whenever she was blocking me, she would find any excuse to touch me, to run her palms down my sweaty chest instead of trying to steal the ball. When she came at me from behind, her hand felt my ass in my shorts. The woman was practically groping me.

I got the ball across the court to a teammate then grabbed her by the hips so she wouldn't run off. I pulled her into me and kissed her while the game continued, tasting her sweat and my own, my hands moving to her ass in her shorts and giving her a good squeeze. When I pulled away, she was a bit paralyzed, so I took off, got the ball, and made a shot without being covered.

She gave me an impish glare then rejoined the game.

After the match was over, when my team won, we headed to the bleachers to cool off and get some water.

She sat beside Charlie, her legs crossed, the towel on her head. "My ass is so sore I can barely sit."

"Want me to massage it for you?" I teased.

"No." She gave me a lighthearted smack. "Well...maybe later."

Charlie cringed before he took a drink from his bottle. "TMI."

"You want to talk about TMI?" she countered. "What about—"

"Do not go there." He silenced her with a look.

"Dirty secret, huh?" I asked.

"He's got a few of them, actually," Carson said. "Let's just say he has sex really loud sometimes..."

He rolled his eyes. "Like you don't..."

"Not with a fifty-year-old," she countered.

"She didn't look fifty," Charlie snapped. "She was the fittest chick I've ever seen."

"And the loudest." She drank from her bottle.

I liked the way they teased each other, like they were really family. I never believed a straight woman and a straight man could be just friends. Sexual attraction and an emotional attachment were inevitable. But somehow, they beat the odds. I wasn't the least bit intimidated by their relationship. Sometimes it felt like Charlie was actually her brother.

"What are we eating?" Matt asked.

"I'll eat anything." Carson pulled the towel off her head and patted her face with it.

"Me too," Charlie said.

"Sandwiches?" I suggested.

"Let's do it." Matt got up first.

I checked in with the guys to see if they wanted to come, but they all had early mornings the next day, so it was just the four of us.

We left the gym and walked down the street together.

"Will William be joining us again?" Carson asked as she walked beside me.

"Maybe. But he's pretty busy." I didn't expect him to join us every week, not when he had a practice to run and patients to see.

"I like him," she said. "He's a cool guy."

"Yeah, I like him too."

We reached the deli and gave our orders. This time, I let her pay for her meal, and I paid for mine—as two separate people. Trying to bind us together at the register was probably the kind of pressure she didn't want.

We sat at the table with chips and sodas and waited for our food.

Carson sat across from me, going to town on her chips. "Your sister hates me...by the way."

I'd never asked Renee how the interview went because I didn't want to talk about Carson. But we also hadn't spent much time together because we were swamped all week. We also worked on different floors, so we didn't see each other unless we went out of our way to do so. "What?"

"That interview did *not* go well." Her hand continued to dive into the chip bag. "Point-blank, she said she didn't like me."

That was shocking to me because I made such an effort with William. "I can't see my sister behaving that way."

"Then ask her." She popped another chip into her mouth. "It was like a scene from *Game of Thrones*. I was Khaleesi, and she was Cersei."

I knew Carson wouldn't lie, but I also couldn't believe my sister would decide to treat her that way.

"So, I don't think she and I will be getting along..." She kept eating.

"No surprise there," Charlie said. "No one likes journalists."

"I didn't ask her anything weird," she countered. "She just came at me hard about Dax."

I couldn't believe Renee did that. Now I knew why she didn't mention it, because she knew I'd be pissed.

Carson finished her bag of chips then eyed mine. "Are you gonna eat that or...?"

Just like that, I forgot I was mad. I tossed the bag to her, a smile on my lips. "All yours, sweetheart."

"Gonna take half his sandwich next?" Charlie turned to me. "Anytime I come to the office with lunch, she takes half of whatever it is. I'm really glad she'll be taking food from you instead of me from now on."

Carson stuck out her tongue. "Maybe I should stop buying groceries for the both of us every week then, huh? Stop buying your damn toilet paper and condoms while I'm at it."

"Ooh..." Matt looked at Charlie. "Don't piss her off."

Carson looked at me. "I just want my man to know I'm not some leech."

My man. I liked that. "You can take all my food if you want. I want my woman to be full and happy."

She stilled at what I said before digging her hand back into the bag and grabbing another chip.

Our sandwiches were brought out, and we ate next to the window.

"I could cry right now," Matt said. "This is so good."

"It's plain turkey and cheese," Charlie said. "It's not even a full sandwich."

Matt spoke with his mouth full. "Don't care...fucking amazing."

Carson had better manners when she ate, but she still inhaled her food like a man.

Charlie finished chewing his bite before he addressed her again. "When are you going to talk to Kat?"

Matt continued to eat, his eyes moving back and forth.

I wasn't sure what Charlie meant exactly.

"You told Matt?" she asked incredulously.

"He's my best friend," Charlie said. "How am I not supposed to tell him?"

"*I'm* your best friend," she argued. "And I don't want Kat or Denise to find out the wrong way."

Matt talked with his mouth full again. "Come on, I would never say anything."

I gathered that Carson had told Charlie the truth about Denise's feelings. I ate as I watched the conversation unfold, enjoying the fact that I was a member of their group instantly, like I belonged there, listening to conversations about people and events, rather than money and corporate greed.

"You're my best *girl* friend—"

"No, bitch." She waved her finger. "I'm your best friend. I don't get demoted because of my coochie."

"Fine," Charlie said. "You're both my best friends. Happy now?"

She grabbed her sandwich again. "It's a little better..."

I turned to Charlie. "Can I be your best friend too?"

He chuckled at my joke. "Sure. Why not?" He turned to Carson. "Seriously, when are you going to talk to her? You and Dax are happy, and there's nothing standing in the way of this conversation."

She gave a loud sigh. "I'll do it in a few days..."

"How about tomorrow?" Charlie pressed.

"Dude, chill." She took another bite of her sandwich. "I'm not going to talk to Kat, have her be cool with it, and then you're going to get laid that night. It's gonna be a lot more complicated than that."

"I don't want to get laid," Charlie argued. "I just want to ask her out."

Matt gave him a skeptical look.

"And if she wanted to do the nasty-nasty…I wouldn't say no." He leaned forward, closer to Carson. "But that's not my goal. I've been into Denise for, like, nine months. I've been waiting for this for a long time."

"But I've got to handle this right, you know?" Carson said. "How this plays out is totally on my shoulders. I don't want to hurt Kat and lose our friendship, but I also want you to fuck my sister and be happy, I want my sister to get some good D… There's a lot going on."

I chuckled at her description.

"I promise, I will talk to her this week," she added.

"Alright." Charlie finally let it go. "You head home right away and tell me everything that happened."

"Fine." She went back to her sandwich and turned to me. "How's your food?"

"Good." I took another bite. "But the view is better."

She rolled her eyes. "I look sooooo bad right now. My hair is greasier than a can of motor oil."

"I think you look cute." I kept eating, my eyes on her. "I like a woman who works up a sweat and gets dirty."

She rolled her eyes again, but she clearly didn't mean it. She liked it when I said things like that, when I complimented her for reasons besides her looks. "And eats like a pig?"

"Yeah, actually."

Charlie watched us. "Carson, you gotta marry this guy, because no other guy is *ever* gonna say that."

FIFTEEN
DAX

I took the elevator to her floor then rang the doorbell twice.

Footsteps sounded after a moment, then my sister checked the peephole. The door opened a second later, and she was in baggy sweatpants that were three times too big, along with a t-shirt. "Dax? What are you doing here?"

"To give you a piece of my mind." I pushed past her and entered the penthouse.

She shut the door. "What are you talking about?"

"Really?" My hands moved to my hips. "You're gonna play stupid right now?"

Her eyes narrowed farther. "You better tread carefully because I'm about to slap the shit out of you."

"Carson told me you ripped her apart in your office." I came closer to her, feeling the rage in my veins.

"What's your point?" She crossed her arms over her chest.

"What's the point?" I asked incredulously. "Why would you treat her like that?"

"Because I don't like her. She's a fucking tease, and she knows it."

Both of my eyebrows rose high on my face. "She's not a tease. And even if she were, how dare you talk to her that way? How would you feel if I treated William like garbage?"

"Totally different. He's not the one who broke my heart."

Footsteps sounded a second later, and William entered the room from the hallway, in jeans and a t-shirt. "Everything alright?"

I didn't think he would be here this late, but then I realized that was a stupid assumption to make. "No, it's not." I turned back to my sister. "Carson and I worked it out. We're together now."

"Really?" Her eyebrows rose. "Then maybe our conversation helped—"

"I doubt it." I was hardly ever angry with her, but right now, I was livid. "I told you about my problems because you said you wanted to have a closer relationship. Everything I said was in confidence. I didn't expect you to launch all that shit at her. It's a fucking betrayal, Renee."

She kept her hostility. "Yes, I was cold, but I also told her she would never find a better man, that you were the best in the world. I told her she'd better make this work because she would regret it for the rest of her life if she didn't. You shouldn't have lied and deceived her, but there's so much more to you than that mistake. I also said all of that, but it looks like it didn't matter to her."

"She told me what happened in a casual context, simply saying you didn't like her and it was like a scene in *Game of Thrones*. She didn't go deeper into it, and honestly, it doesn't seem like she cares whether you like her or not. But I still can't believe you came at her like that, especially when I still wanted her, even then."

She finally bowed her head. "Look, I wasn't planning on saying any of that. But when I looked at her...it just came out. It's hard to be around someone who's hurting your brother. How would you feel if I asked you to be around William after he hurt me?"

"I wouldn't like it, but I wouldn't lose my shit either."

"It sounds like there's no harm done anyway, if she doesn't care."

"That's not the point." I pointed at her. "You shouldn't have done that."

"And I apologized—"

"No, you didn't," I snapped.

Her eyes fell in guilt. "Okay...I'm sorry."

"I'm really going out of my way to have a relationship with William, and I'd appreciate a change in attitude so you can do the same."

"I don't see how the relationships are the same. William and I are serious and—"

"She's the one."

Renee stopped her argument, dropped her attitude. Her arms slackened and fell to her sides. Now her eyes looked at me differently, like she was really hearing me for the first time.

"Make this right, Renee."

As if she couldn't speak, she gave a nod.

SHE OPENED THE DOOR. "Ooh, you brought beer."

I stepped inside and greeted her with a kiss.

She melted at my touch, just the way she used to, but with more potency.

I moved past her and carried the beer to the fridge. "Where are the guys?"

"Getting the pizza."

"No delivery?" I met her at the dining table.

"It's cheaper," she said. "And Charlie is still at the office."

I twisted off the cap of my beer, took a drink, and set it down.

"How was your day?"

"Boring."

"I doubt being a CEO is boring."

"Let me paint a picture for you." I came closer to her, feeling that energy that bounced back and forth between us. "Do you have meetings at work?"

"Yes. Weekly."

"Do you enjoy them?"

She shrugged.

"Well, imagine you're in a meeting all day, every day."

"Sounds terrible, but I don't see how that's possible."

"That's what I do, handle one meeting then the next—over and over."

"You're right...that is boring."

Fall was almost here, so her little shorts and tanks were starting to disappear. Now she was in jeans more often, along with a blouse. But whether she was in sweaty gym clothes or black lingerie, she was gorgeous. Right now, with her bright eyes and subtle smile, she was really something.

I stared at her for a while before the urge overtook me. There were so many times when I wanted to do this but couldn't because there was an invisible barrier between us. I moved into her, my arms circling her petite body, and I held her close to me.

It was just a hug, but it felt so damn good.

My chin rested on her head, and my hand dug into her hair as I cradled her close, my other arm around her waist. I closed my eyes as I held her, my fingers stroking slightly, and I smelled her hair, felt her presence wrap around mine.

Her arms curled around my waist, and she rested against me, like the affection was just as addictive to her. She inhaled a deep breath then went still, just holding me, letting me hold her.

After a few minutes passed, I pulled away.

She released me, but reluctantly.

I pulled out a folded piece of paper from my pocket and left it on the table.

"What's this?" She grabbed it and opened it.

"I'm in no rush. I just want you to know where I stand." Whenever it was time for us to be together, I wasn't wearing a condom. Condoms were for one-night stands and partners who didn't mean anything. That didn't apply to us at all. If she wasn't ready for that kind of intimacy, I would wait. I'd rather wait for the real thing than settle for less.

She folded the paper then slipped it into her pocket.

I sat down at the table and drank my beer.

She sat down too. She was usually quick with the words, but when it was just us, she had less to say. I loved hearing every thought in her mind, but I loved the silence too, as if our relationship had deepened so words weren't required to have a connection.

"Can I ask you something?"

She gave a slight nod. "Anything."

I liked that answer. "Was that the first time you've seen him?"

She seemed to understand exactly who I was asking about. "The last time I saw him was over a year ago. We signed the divorce papers, then I grabbed a couple things that were still in the apartment. And that was it."

"You haven't spoken?"

She shook her head.

When I'd kissed her, I'd done it because I didn't want her to focus on the past, to think about the lies of omission that demolished her heart. I wanted her to focus on the man who would do anything to have her, that I was her future and not a repeat of the past. It was different with us, and that kiss was enough proof that we had something real. I didn't spend a lot of time kissing women. It happened, but it always accelerated into something more sexual. But with her, a kiss was sexual enough. "Is he married to the woman he left you for?"

"I would assume so, but I really have no idea. I don't stalk him online or anything." Her hand moved to the table, and she beckoned to me with her fingers.

I pushed the beer to her, like I was the bartender and she was a cowboy in a bar.

She took a drink then pushed it back.

I caught it and steadied it before it tipped over. "Do you want to talk about it?" I wanted to know how she felt in her own words, but I didn't want to push her into something she didn't want to do.

She looked away and gave a shrug. "Not much to say. When I first saw him and spotted his wedding ring, I did feel terrible. It was like he'd cut me again, in the same place where he'd done it before, sliced right through the scar tissue. And that pain isn't because I still had any affection for him. It was just because it reminded me that I never mattered, that he never really loved me, that it was all just a big mistake... and he never cared for me. It made me feel like shit that I didn't realize it as it happened, that I didn't see the signs, that I didn't question his actions or behaviors. I was totally blind. It's just humiliating, you know?"

"Yeah, I do know." I didn't want her to know the pain of a bad relationship, but it did make me connect to her better, because she knew exactly how it felt to be used and spat out.

"But when you walked to me, I knew what was about to happen. It was like a long pause, where time stood still, where everything became quiet. And then you kissed me... and I forgot about everything else. Evan left my thoughts, and I didn't think about him again. All I thought about was you. Couldn't care less if Evan saw me or not. Couldn't care less if it bothered him or not. It just...felt right. It grounded me, pulled me to the present, showed me that I was exactly where I was supposed to be."

My face remained stoic, but those words burned me from the inside out, made me feel alive and dead at the same time. This deep connection I felt for her was reciprocated, and she was finally allowing herself to feel everything she was afraid of. She was giving herself to me, handing over pieces of her heart, one at a time. My lie had ruined what we'd been developing, but we came back stronger than before, because what we had...was real.

Charlie and Matt walked inside with the pizza. "Why isn't the TV on?" Charlie barked.

I ignored them and continued to stare at her, holding on to that emotion a little longer before the energy turned casual and the moment was gone entirely.

She stared at me too, as if she wasn't quite ready to let go.

"Oh, sweet." Charlie carried the pizzas to the dining table and placed them in between us. "You brought beer. Thanks, man." He headed into the kitchen to grab the plates.

"No problem," I said, still looking at Carson.

Charlie and Matt came to the table and started pulling the pieces out of the box between us.

"Did you talk to Kat?" Charlie asked.

She tilted her head back and sighed. "I will tell you when I do, alright?"

"But when?" Charlie pressed. "You said you were doing it this week."

"We're having dinner tomorrow," Carson said. "So chill."

"About fucking time." Charlie shoved a slice into his mouth and headed to the couch.

"You gonna eat?" Matt handed me a plate.

"Sure." I took it.

"What about me?" Carson said in offense. "I feel like you've replaced me with Dax."

"We have," Charlie said from his spot on the couch facing the TV.

"He's much better." When Matt had all his pizza, he headed to the couch to join Charlie.

She looked at me and shook her head.

I stood up and set my plate in front of her. "Here, sweetheart."

She took the plate with a slight smile. "At least someone here likes me."

WHEN THE GAME WAS OVER, Matt left. "See ya."

"Bye." Charlie carried the plates to the sink then put all the empty bottles into the recycling.

I didn't expect to stay, but I also didn't want to leave either.

When he was finished, he headed down the hallway. "Night, Dax."

"Night, man."

Carson sat on the other couch, and she watched him leave the room with her arms raised. "Uh, bye?"

Charlie shut his door in response.

"He teases you because he loves you." I leaned forward with my arms on my knees. "It's one of the perks of being so close to someone."

"I wouldn't call it a perk..." She got to her feet and grabbed the remote to turn off the TV.

I knew I wouldn't get an invitation to stay, so I rose to my feet and headed to the door.

She followed me, coming close to me and immediately circling her arms around my waist as I turned to face her. Her eyes went to my lips, like she wanted to kiss me all over, but she didn't. Her eyes flicked back to mine.

My arms wrapped around her, and I held her with the same enthusiasm, wanting to drag my hands all over her body and feel the curves my fingers could never forget. All the other women in my bed were a disappointment because they didn't have what she did. She was fucking perfect.

"I'd ask you to stay, but..." Her eyes lifted from my mouth to my eyes.

"There's no rush, sweetheart." My hand cupped her face, and I kissed her, getting a taste of what we could have whenever she was ready to give me all of her, not just a piece. She used to use sex as a distraction, a meaningless act to cure the loneliness while guarding her heart. But now that she was emotionally available, it actually meant something to her, and that was exactly what I wanted. I wanted her, all of her—heart, body, and soul. "You're worth the wait."

SIXTEEN

CARSON

"So, how are things with Dax?" Kat sat across from me and waggled her eyebrows. We got a drink after work and split an appetizer. "Girl…that kiss." She licked her lips. "You're a lucky woman, I'll say that." She grabbed her lemon drop and took a drink.

"Yeah, he's good at the kissing thing."

"He's good at everything, right?"

"Yes." I hadn't had it in a while, but my memory hadn't faded. But I also suspected the sex would be totally different…whenever it happened.

"Are you guys doing it all over the place?"

"Well, we haven't gotten there yet."

"What?" she asked in surprise. "If you aren't screwing, what are you doing?"

I shrugged. "Talking and stuff…"

She stared at me like I was the biggest weirdo she'd ever met. "Who are you right now? You went from juggling boy toys and playing the field to being in a monogamous relationship without sex?"

"We're just taking it slow."

"But you've already slept together."

"I know. But it's different…"

She drank her lemon drop and narrowed her eyes, like she wanted me to elaborate.

"Come on, everyone knows I was sleeping around as a defense mechanism. I was coping in the only way I knew how. But I don't want to do that with Dax. When I sleep with him, it's going to be…different. It's gonna be meaningful. That's just a lot for me right now, and I'm not sure if I'm ready."

"You mean you're going to make love instead of fuck?"

"I guess. And I haven't done that since I was married…"

Her eyes softened once she understood. "That's pretty romantic, actually."

"I really like him, and while I'm fucking terrified, I want to do this. I want to have a relationship. You know…a deep one. I'm not even angry with him anymore for the lie he fed me. I'm just…totally hung up on him. I hate it, but I am."

She gave me a slight smile. "I think this is great. You know, it means you've really moved on, emotionally."

"Not quite…because I have to sleep with him still."

"Come on, it's going to be amazing."

"Yeah, I'm sure it will."

She drank from her glass again then moved to the nachos. "I'm happy for you. I know Dax was a little shady in the beginning, but you can tell he's a good man. Come on, a man doesn't kiss like that unless he's totally sprung."

It was a damn good kiss.

She kept picking at the nachos.

We did the small-talk thing, caught up, discussed work, and our relationships...and now there was nothing else to talk about.

That meant I had to do the thing I absolutely didn't want to do. "Kat...there's something I want to talk about."

"Alright..." She grabbed another chip and popped it into her mouth, but her eyes were narrowed on my face, anticipating the fall. "Lay it on me, girl."

"Well, it's kinda a rough thing to talk about. I wasn't going to say anything, but I felt like I should. So, here it goes..."

"Now I'm officially freaked out."

"Denise told me she kinda has a thing for Charlie." I started with my sister since the truth about Charlie would hurt a lot more. "They've been spending time together, and she said she's attracted to him...thinks he's great."

Her eyes dropped, and the blood drained from her face, like this really stung her. She had been about to grab another chip but dropped her hand instead. "Um..." She released a heavy sigh. "I'm trying to be diplomatic about this whole thing since she's your sister...but that's a knife right in my back. There are rules for these things. What kind of friend is she?"

"Before you get mad, she said she would never do anything because of your friendship."

Relief flashed across her eyes, her temper dimmed. "Good. Charlie and I were together for years, and we've only been broken up for nine months… That would be just callous."

I found it ironic that she hadn't gotten over their relationship, but people expected me just to bounce back after my divorce when I'd had almost the same amount of time to digest it. "Yeah."

"Thanks for telling me…I guess."

"Well, I wouldn't have said anything at all because there's no point. If she's not going to do anything, then it doesn't matter. But…Charlie told me he has feelings for her."

Now, she truly looked distraught, the light leaving her eyes as the hope drained from her face. Her gaze dropped, she took a deep breath, and she looked devastated, her fingers fidgeting with her hair.

I hated this, so much. "I'm sorry, Kat. I'm so sorry…"

She wouldn't look at me, like if she did, she would start to cry. "What did he say…exactly?"

"I guess he's felt this way for a while…but he would never do anything because of the situation."

Her eyes stayed down. "I…I thought we might get back together. He broke up with me so suddenly, and I thought he would realize it was a mistake and come back… But he doesn't feel that way at all, does he?"

I didn't want to lie and give her false hope, but I didn't want to tell the truth and crush her spirit either.

She lifted her gaze and looked at me, like a frightened animal.

"No..."

She inhaled a deep breath, her eyes slowly starting to well up. "Oh fuck..." She dropped her gaze again and looked at the table so she could control her emotions.

My hand moved to hers on the table, and I squeezed her fingers.

She sniffled then grabbed the cocktail napkin to dab the corners of her eyes.

I knew she still cared about him, but I hadn't understood how deeply until now. "I thought things were going well with Nathan?"

"I mean...they're fine. We're having fun. But...that's it." She pulled her hand away from mine.

"Just because Nathan isn't the right one doesn't mean the next guy won't be. Kat, you're amazing. You're going to find an amazing guy who will love you so much he can't imagine his life without you." She was so gorgeous, so fun, so interesting. I knew Charlie's feelings for Denise were strong if he would walk away from Kat without looking back. So, they just weren't meant to be.

"I know, but I really loved Charlie. When I pictured myself in a wedding dress, he was the man watching me walk down the aisle."

Now I wished Denise had never relocated here. I wished I weren't having this conversation. I wished I didn't have to watch my best friend get crushed the way Evan crushed me. "I know, girl..."

She grabbed her drink and finished the rest of it. After a few deep breaths, she calmed herself, cleansed her emotions, and stared out the window somberly. "I guess I really need to move on...because it's not going to happen."

"Yeah."

She turned back to me. "I guess I needed to know the truth...as much as it hurts, so I can have closure and move on."

I respected her attitude. She was strong. "So...you think I should tell them about the other's feelings and give them your blessing?"

She looked totally caught off guard. "What?"

"You know...because they want to be together."

"You're serious right now?" She cocked her head and turned vicious. "They should be together while I just stand there and watch? That's completely inappropriate. She's my friend, he's the guy I'm still in love with, you're my best friend... That just sounds like a fucking nightmare."

I'd hoped this wouldn't be her reaction, but she was emotional and upset, and she wasn't ready. "So, I should just keep it to myself?"

"Yes. We were together for two years. How could anyone expect me to just shrug it off and be okay with it?"

If she knew Charlie's feelings were much deeper, she might have a change of heart, but I could never tell her that...because that would be too much.

"Absolutely not. You take that shit to the grave."

I didn't react to her words, didn't show my disappointment. "Alright."

She grabbed my drink and took a sip.

"I just think...if you really care about Charlie...you would want him to be happy." He'd been feeling this way for Denise for a long time, but he didn't do anything about it out of respect for Kat's feelings. He even ended their relationship because he didn't want to lie to her, pretend those feelings didn't exist when he was strongly attracted to someone else. He did every honorable thing possible.

"Of course. He meets someone and falls in love and proposes...I would understand. I would be happy for him, even if it hurt. But to have to watch him be with my friend and have to look at it all the time...that's rough. Because we're always hanging out, so they'll always be together. It'll literally be in my face all the time. No, I can't do that." She shook her head. "Could you?"

If I had to see Dax with Denise, it would kill me. When she'd made a comment about having him, it had made me possessive when he wasn't even mine. It would be difficult to be in those shoes and deal with that pain every day. It would be difficult for anyone, almost too much to ask. But I knew I would, because it was the right thing to do. "Hard to say..."

INSTEAD OF HEADING BACK to the apartment to talk to Charlie, I texted Dax. *I need you.* Charlie wouldn't text or call out of fear that Kat would see his message, so I wouldn't have to deal with him until I walked in the door. So, I wanted to avoid that as long as possible. I wasn't the one with a broken heart, but I was devastated, and I reached out to Dax like a lifeline...which was a first.

He texted me back instantly. *Sweetheart, I'm here. What do you need?*

Can I come over?

Always.

I walked a few blocks to his penthouse, checked in with security, and rode the elevator to his floor. His whole world was vastly different from mine, but instead of seeing him as some rich suit, I saw him as Dax...the man. The doors opened and revealed him standing there, in just his sweatpants. His expression was focused on mine, his eyebrows rigid, his jaw clenched tightly, like my well-being was the single most important thing in the world to him. He cared about every emotion I felt, volunteered to carry my baggage like he wanted to be miserable with me rather than happy alone.

I moved into his chest and rested my face against his hardness, feeling those thick arms wrap around me like armor. He pulled me closer, his chin resting on my head, his arms squeezing me tightly. He didn't flood me with a million questions. He gave me all the time I needed, provided silent comfort that was better than a long-winded conversation.

I already felt better.

I pulled my head back, feeling him brush his lips across my forehead and kiss me before he loosened his hold on my body. "Talk to me."

"I just had dinner with Kat."

Understanding entered his gaze as his hands slid down my arms until they released me altogether.

"She was so hurt...devastated."

His eyes softened.

"And I hated doing that to her, hurting her like that." Making your best friend cry was the worst feeling in the world. I wished Charlie had never met Denise, that this whole thing had never happened. I had to do the dirty work because I was the only one who could make it as painless as possible.

His arm circled my waist again, slipping underneath my shirt to my bare back as he guided me to the couch.

I took a seat, kicked off my shoes, and tucked my feet against my ass.

He sat beside me, his large hand moving to my thigh, his gaze on me.

My arm hooked through his while my other hand rested on his sculpted forearm. His skin was so warm to the touch, and while his hard body was irresistible in that moment, I couldn't really appreciate it. "I asked if I could tell Charlie and Denise how the other feels, but she said no."

He didn't pass judgment or give a reaction. He just watched me.

"When I go home, Charlie is gonna be sitting there waiting for me, and I have to tell him what Kat said, which will disappoint him and make her look bad. This just sucks. I hate it."

His fingers gripped my thighs gently, his fingers stroking me through my jeans. "Give her more time. You dropped a lot of information on her at once. Let her sleep on it for a bit."

"Yeah…"

"It made her emotional, so she reacted emotionally. Don't judge her for that."

I nodded. "I understand. I mean, she's still in love with him, so of course this hurts. And no one wants to watch their ex, who they are in love with, be in love with a friend…all the time. It's totally reasonable."

"It is."

"I wish Denise had never moved here. I love my sister and I'm happy I see her all the time, but life would be much easier if she'd stayed put."

"Maybe."

I looked up to meet his gaze.

His scruff was coming in thick, matching the color of his eyes. "But if these two are meant to be together, it had to happen."

"It's too early to tell."

"But if there's a chance…any chance at all…"

I rested my face on his shoulder.

His lips kissed my hairline. "I know things are rough right now, but they'll get better…eventually."

"Or I could just stay here and never deal with it at all."

He chuckled quietly, his breath floating over my forehead. "I'd love that."

"No, you wouldn't." I stared down his hard body, seeing the flat abs that went all the way down to the top of his sweatpants. The dramatic lines formed a V shape that I wanted to trace with my fingertips. "I'd eat all your food, get popcorn in the crevices, drink all your beer. Charlie has warned you extensively."

"I can handle it."

I pulled away so I could look at his expression instead of his perfect body. "I don't know...Charlie knows me better than anyone, and he can't."

"I'm a bigger man than he is."

I gave a slight smile then glided my fingers over his chest, feeling all the hard muscle. The attraction was there, and I wanted to drag my tongue from the bottom of his abs, all the way up his neck, and then to his sexy jawline. I wanted to stick my hand down his bottoms and rub his dick as I tasted his skin. But those urges would have to wait.

He must have read the desire in my eyes, because his hand dug deep into my hair and pinned it back from my face, his eyes looking at my lips.

My heart stopped beating.

He stared at me for a while before he pulled me into him, guiding my mouth to his, his hand fisting my hair harder, getting a strong hold of it.

Once our mouths were connected, my thighs squeezed together and a breath escaped my lips. My nails instinctively dug into his chest, clawing into his flesh. I stared into his eyes as I kissed him, but then they closed when the passion made my hands shake. It was like the kiss in the bar, but a million times stronger, a fire that grew into an inferno.

He breathed into my mouth between kisses, his mouth turning to the other side before he gave me some tongue. When he felt them circle together, he released a quiet moan, his fingers clenching deeper in my hair.

My hands explored his body, moving all the way down over his stomach, across the hard abs I wanted to lick. My fingers ached to go farther to feel his big dick, but I stayed above the waist.

He started to guide me back to the couch to move on top of me.

My hand slid back to his chest, and I steadied him, our lips breaking apart, our eyes locking together with lidded gazes. "I...I don't trust myself." If I let his muscular body lie on top of mine, I would pull down his bottoms and get mine off soon after. It would turn into a moment I wasn't ready to have, and we'd rushed too quickly last time and destroyed the entire thing in the process.

He cradled my head and stared at my mouth. "But you can trust me."

My hand slid down his chest again, toward his stomach.

"I want that moment when it's perfect, when you're ready to have me the way I'm ready to have you." His eyes moved to mine. "So, you don't need to worry about it going somewhere it's not supposed to go. It'll be what it's supposed to be." He looked at my lips again, as if asking for permission.

He'd rushed me last time, but he was determined not to rush me again, to let me have exactly what I wanted. That made me trust him, despite his lies. It made me believe this could really be the right thing, because the finish line was in sight, so there was no need to sprint to it.

I nestled back into him and let my lips land on his.

He inhaled a deep breath as he kissed me, his hand fisting my hair once again, his strong body guiding me backward as he moved on top of me. His thighs separated mine so he could fit on top of me easier.

My ankles locked together around his waist, and I dug my fingers into his hair, my kisses increasing in intensity right away, becoming more carnal, more aggressive. My hand snaked up his back and dug into his skin, clawing at it like he was inside me, making me writhe.

His passion matched mine, and even though this wouldn't end up with us in bed together or our clothes on the floor, he was just as excited, like the moment was enough for him.

His mouth left mine and lowered to my jawline and neck, placing his kisses all over my body, moving to the collar of my shirt without going further. His teeth gently bit at my collarbone before he rose back up again, kissing me hard, like he wanted all of me, every single piece.

It was the most passionate moment of my life, feeling him kiss me like that, want me like that. Lust was sharp in my touch, digging into his flesh, but it was more than that, a sensation in my chest, a closeness of our souls that I could feel distinctly. Emotional and deep, it was more than just a make-out session on the couch.

A lot more.

IT WAS ALMOST ten when I walked in the door.

Charlie jumped up from the couch, the spot where he'd been waiting all night. "What happened? What did she say?"

Dax had chased away all my problems with his affection and powerful kiss, but now that I was back in the apartment, reality had returned. Now that Charlie was staring at me with the expectant expression, I wished I'd just spent the night. "It was rough, Charlie."

He walked past the couches and joined me in the entryway. "At least it's over, right?"

It was far from over.

"Did she give her blessing?"

I understood Kat's position, it was totally reasonable, but I hoped she'd change her mind. "I need more time with her."

Defeat started to creep into his face. "Then it was really rough..."

"You have no idea." I walked past him. "I'll work on it."

He followed after me. "So...is she okay?"

I turned back around. "What do you expect, Charlie? The woman is still in love with you, and I had to tell her you had a thing for my sister and my sister has a thing for you. She hoped you would get back together at some point. She thought you still had a chance. So yeah, she's fucking devastated."

It seemed like he genuinely cared about her pain, the way his eyes dropped and he quietly sighed. "Jesus..."

"Yeah. Jesus," I snapped. "Ugh, I wish my sister had never moved here. I wish none of this was happening. I wish I didn't have to break my best friend's heart again when you already broke it."

He raised his hand. "I get that you're upset, but stop yelling at me."

I crossed my arms over my chest and forced myself to calm. "I just... This really sucks."

"I know it does." He walked back toward me, his eyes sympathetic. "I appreciate you doing this, helping me like this." His hands went to my arms, and he gave me a gentle squeeze. "I don't want to hurt Kat. I'll always love her...in a way. I wish she were head over heels for Nathan and I was the last thing on her mind. But I can't put my life on hold forever. I've waited as long as I can. This is complicated and painful, but it had to happen."

I nodded. "She did say it's given her the closure she needs. Now that she knows it's never going to happen."

"Then maybe some good will come out of this."

"But she also said she couldn't handle seeing the two of you together, if that ever happens. We all hang out together all the time, so it would always be in her face...and it would be too hard."

He rubbed his hands up and down my arms. "Yeah, I get it."

"But I'll give her some time to process what I said—"

"Maybe I should talk to her now."

"What?" I whispered. "I think that will just make it worse. You're going to try to convince her to be okay with your infatuation with my sister? No. That's not going to work, Charlie. Just give me some more time."

He dropped his hands. "Alright." His eyes remained on my face, looking at my features, particularly my lips.

"What?"

His eyes narrowed. "Your lips look all weird."

My fingers brushed across the bottom lip, feeling the slight puffiness. "Dax and I...kissed for a bit on his couch."

"A bit?" He grinned. "That had to be at least an hour's worth of kissing...hard kissing."

"Well, he's a good kisser." I dropped my fingers.

"So...you guys do the deed?"

"No. Just kissed."

His eyebrow rose. "You guys made out on the couch, hard, for an hour and didn't sleep together?"

"Taking it slow. I've done the fuck-a-thon thing already. I want it to be different this time."

His smile remained, but his eyes softened. "That makes me really happy." His arms circled my waist, and he brought me close, his chin moving to my head, his arms feeling like home. "You're back..."

SEVENTEEN
DAX

I sat at my desk and grabbed my phone. With a smile on my face, I texted Carson. *Can I take you to dinner tonight?* I'd avoided asking her on a date because that seemed like too much, too fast. But it felt right now...after our passionate interlude on my couch. That happened days ago, but I hadn't stopped thinking about it.

Hadn't stopped smiling.

She texted back. *Yes.*

I read that response three times.

Another message popped up. *But I have one condition.*

Name it.

Nowhere fancy. I want a hot dog or something.

My grin widened. *Got it. Nothing fancy. But a hot dog? Really?*

Are you telling me you don't hit up the food carts on the street?

If I did, would I look like this? *Not really.*

Fine. No hot dogs. But something at that level.

How about that Chinese place we went to last time?

Peeeeerfect.

I chuckled. *See you then, sweetheart.* I set my phone to the side.

It vibrated again. *By the way, I got flowers today.*

Well, they weren't from me. *Yeah?*

Your sister sent them.

Good. Finally mending the relationship she destroyed.

Said she was sorry about our last meeting. But that was totally unnecessary. She's free to dislike me all she wants. I don't care.

I liked her no-bullshit attitude. She was confident and unbreakable. *I told her we've reconciled, so now she has no reason to dislike you.*

Then they are even more unnecessary. But they're beautiful and they're a nice accent to my desk, so tell her I said thank you.

I will. I set the phone down.

Minutes later, Renee walked inside. "Your ex-wife is a real peach."

Nothing could sabotage my mood, not even Rose. "Yeah?"

"She's here, you know, causing destruction."

"Lovely..."

She tossed some papers onto the desk.

I kept my stare on her face.

With one hand on her hip, she stared at me. "You look creepy when you smile like that."

"Creepy? I have a nice smile."

"But when it's constant, it's just weird. Why are you smiling anyway?"

I wasn't going to tell her about the session on the couch, the way we collided passionately like we were making love. Her nails anchored into my back and left marks that were still there. She bruised my lips with her aggressive embraces. Her hands were all over me, in my hair, on my shoulders, scratching down my chest. She writhed underneath me without even needing my dick. I was more than enough. "She just told me about the flowers you sent."

"Oh, good. I'm glad she liked them."

"Yeah."

"So, did that fix it?"

"She didn't have any ill feelings toward you, so I guess there was nothing to fix."

"Then, my job is done?" she asked.

"Not quite. What if the four of us go to dinner?"

"Really?" She cocked her head to the side.

It was a little soon to do a family dinner, but since Carson had already met Renee and William, I didn't see the harm. "She already likes William, so that shouldn't be a problem. And I know you would like her if you got to know her."

"The smile you've been wearing for days already makes me like her, Dax."

Good answer.

"She just needed to pull her head out of her ass. It's okay, we've all been there. Just let me know where and when."

"Got it."

She turned to leave. "And get those papers signed by the end of the day."

CHARLIE OPENED THE DOOR. "HEY, MAN."

I walked inside and greeted him with a grip of our hands.

"What brings you here?"

"Taking Carson out."

"Oh, like a date?" He shut the door then faced me.

"Yeah."

He smiled. "Good. Just don't take her anywhere nice. She hates pretentious food."

"Yeah, I figured that out," I said with a chuckle. "We're going to a Chinese place."

"Perfect." He gave me a thumbs-up. "Maybe have another make-out session afterward."

"She told you that?"

"Man, she tells me everything, and I mean *everything*."

"Good to know," I said with another chuckle.

"She seems pretty happy. Has nothing but good things to say."

"Yeah. I'm really happy too."

He glanced toward the hallway to make sure she wasn't there. "She told me she wants to wait because she wants it to be different with you."

I knew I was getting a version of Carson I'd never met before, someone without walls, someone without fear. She was giving me her heart, piece by piece. She didn't want me because I was hot or had a big dick. She wanted me on a much deeper level, just like it'd been on the couch. "It already is different." Based on that kiss, she was ready. Ready to give all of herself to me, to make love to me. But I'd let her realize that on her own.

He gave me a clap on my shoulder. "You want a beer?"

"No. I'm sure she'll be—"

"God, I'm hungry." She came down the hallway in jeans and a blouse, her long hair in curls, her makeup dark and sultry. She looked like fire, dancing flames. She grabbed her purse from the table and walked up to me, her eyes light with affection, like she couldn't wait to reach me.

My arms circled her waist, and I gave her a kiss. My hands snaked down and gave both of her cheeks a manly squeeze.

"You enjoy your dinner." Charlie walked away. "I'm just going to go throw up."

As if she didn't hear a word he said, she pulled away and looked into my face with a pretty smile. "Ready?"

"Yeah."

We left the apartment and headed to the sidewalk.

I grabbed her hand and locked our fingers together.

She turned to me, a slight smile on her lips.

This was what I wanted, what I'd wanted since the moment I set eyes on her. I didn't miss the strippers or the strangers in the bars. I wanted this, even though I'd thought I wasn't ready to have this ever again. But she didn't care about my money. She didn't want to go to a fancy restaurant and watch me drop a thousand dollars on a single meal. She didn't even ask me about that sort of thing.

It was exactly what I wanted.

We reached the Chinese restaurant and took a seat at a small table, the same one we had last time, right up against the window.

"If we're going to get hot and heavy again, I'll skip the spicy stuff."

She looked at her menu, a smile moving onto her lips. "Good thinking. I'll get the chicken lo mein."

"Me too."

The waitress came over, and we ordered drinks and our food at the same time.

"When am I going to see that article?" My elbows were on the table with my hands together, and she did the same thing, leaning forward like she was trying to get to me, and I was trying to get to her.

"I'm done with it."

"Yeah?"

She nodded. "You want to read it first before I publish it?"

"I trust you'll make me look good."

She chuckled. "Vince had me rewrite a couple things because he said there was an obvious bias to it..."

"What kind of bias?"

"That I think you're sexy and charming."

"Well, I am those things, so that's fair."

She laughed. "Now I need to go back and add arrogant."

"Also true, so also fair."

"It'll probably run on Friday. I'll let you know."

"I'll grab a copy so you can sign it."

"I'm not a novelist," she said with a chuckle.

"You're still a writer. I'll frame it and put it on the wall."

She didn't say anything, but her eyes gave away her feelings. My support of her career clearly meant a lot to her. It was her passion, not just her job, and compliments were a big deal.

I hated the danger her job put her in, but I didn't know what the solution was. If I asked her to stop, she would never agree. And if I asked...she would probably dump me. She didn't seem like a woman who would want to be with a man who would ask her such a thing. So I just had to keep my mouth shut...and pray nothing ever happened to her.

"What's new with you at the office?"

I shrugged. "Meetings...and meetings."

"Come on, that can't be true. Based on what you told me, you're pretty involved in product development."

"Which is done through meetings..."

She chuckled.

"That is the part of my job I enjoy the most. I enjoy steering the guys in development. If I had the skills or the intelligence, I'd probably move down there and actually work alongside them."

"You definitely have the intelligence. Maybe you just need to acquire the skills. Have your sister take your position, and you move downstairs."

"Always an idea."

The food arrived, and Carson immediately dug in. She must have noticed my stare because she offered an explanation. "I didn't have lunch today. I was running all over the place, and Charlie didn't have any food when I came back."

"How are things with Charlie?"

"He was disappointed by Kat's response but also sympathetic to the situation. I've been giving Kat some space..."

"Probably a good idea."

She stabbed her fork into the noodles, spun them around, and then placed everything into her mouth in a big bite.

"I was thinking we could have dinner with my sister and William this Friday."

She slowly chewed her food, her eyes on me. When she got everything down, she still took a bit to respond. "Is there a reason why?"

"I just thought it would be nice if you and my sister started over."

She took another bite.

I hoped this wasn't pushing her too much, but I'd been optimistic about a more positive response. "If you aren't ready for that—"

"No," she said. "Let's do it."

Her response was a relief. "You already know William and you've met Renee, so I didn't think it would be a serious thing."

"It's fine. It'll be fun."

I really loved this new version of her, a woman who wasn't ready to run the second any kind of commitment was put on the table. She was giving her entire effort this time, wanted us to be together for the long haul. "Renee told me she likes you."

"What?" She stopped before placing another bite into her mouth. "How can that be? You should have seen the way she ripped into me, which is fine. She was just protecting her brother. If some girl were hurting Charlie, I'd probably go full Cersei on her too."

"Because I've been really happy, and she knows that's because of you."

She continued to eat, but there was a softness to her eyes, an affectionate haze to her features that showed how much that meant to her. "I've been really happy too...and that's because of you."

I WALKED her back to her apartment, but I hoped the night wouldn't end on the doorstep.

She got the door unlocked and opened it, but Charlie was sitting on the couch, so she closed it again to say goodbye.

I didn't want to walk away and sleep alone. I wanted to feel her back against my chest, listen to her breathe as I fell asleep. I wanted her hair all over the place, even in my face, her smell heavy in my nose.

"Thanks for dinner." Her hands moved to my stomach before slowly gliding up.

"Thanks for letting me pay for it."

The corner of her mouth rose in a smile. "I get to pay next time."

"Alright." I knew she would never change, that she didn't want me to pay for everything every time we went out. That just wasn't who she was, and while I didn't want her to spend her money on me, I wanted to respect her wishes, even though it was hard sometimes.

"Well...goodnight." She was in her flats, so she had to rise on her tiptoes and grip my shoulders to kiss me.

I pulled her into me and balanced her as I kissed her, giving her a goodbye kiss instead of a heated embrace. But her lips were so soft and full...and she was such a good kisser. She knew how to give and take, let me have her all I wanted before she reciprocated.

She moved away and lowered her feet to the floor.

It was impossible to leave her. "Can I stay over?" The words came out of my mouth easily, of their own accord. I didn't want anything physical from her, just to feel her soul wrap around mine like it had on the couch.

Her eyes shifted back and forth as she looked into mine.

"Just to sleep." My hand moved into her hair, keeping it back from her face.

She gave a slight nod. "Okay..." She turned back to the door and walked inside.

We moved past the living room and headed for the hallway.

Charlie ignored us, watching TV with a beer in hand.

We entered her bedroom.

My eyes immediately went to the headboard, where I'd secured her wrists and took her hard. Bondage wasn't particularly my thing, but when she asked me to do it, it was the hottest thing in the world.

My dick got hard at the memory.

But I pushed the thought away because that wasn't what I wanted to do now.

Her fingers went to the bottom of my shirt and slowly pulled it over my head.

I let her undress me, felt the cotton move over my head and tug on my hair. My heart started to race a little because it was hot, watching her remove my shirt.

Instead of dropping it to the floor, she held it in her hands. "Do you mind if I wear this?"

And then she made it even hotter. "No."

She moved toward the door. "I'm going to brush my teeth and wash my face. I'll be back."

"Alright." I watched her go until the door was closed behind her. I wasn't sleeping in jeans, so I took them off and left my phone on her other nightstand so it would be within my reach. I changed my alarm to go off a little earlier than usual, so I had time to head back to my penthouse and get ready for the day.

I pulled back her covers and lay there, looking through the blinds of the closed window.

She returned minutes later, her face free of makeup, her hair having a kink in it because it'd been in a ponytail in the bathroom. My shirt was almost to her knees, practically a potato sack on her, but she looked sexier in that than she did in the black lingerie.

With one hand behind my head, I stared at her, watched her walk into the room, gorgeous in makeup and just as gorgeous without it. She turned off the lamp then got into bed beside me.

Once she was under the covers, I turned to face her, pulling her leg over my hip, bringing us close together, her chest to mine, our heads on the same pillow. It was so comfortable, like we fit together perfectly despite our height differences. My hand slid underneath the shirt and up her bare back, finding the ideal place to rest against her spine.

I stared at her beautiful face in the dark, the light from the cracks in the blinds coming in and hitting parts of her cheek. The entire thing was a turn-on because this was the most desirable woman in the world, but my dick remained soft because my pure intentions overrode my biological reaction. I didn't want more than this. It was more than enough, gave me more satisfaction than the hard sex we used to have. She was far more beautiful like this, free of makeup, her heart on her sleeve instead of locked behind a cage.

Her arm slid around my torso, her hand against my back. Her eyes moved down to my lips, but she didn't kiss me. She stayed still, fought the same urges I felt.

"Goodnight, sweetheart." My hand glided up until I brushed the hair out of her face, my fingers keeping it pinned back as they slid farther into the curtain of softness. I closed my eyes a moment later, feeling the peace I'd been searching for my entire life. It was the first relationship I'd had with anyone where I didn't have to question why they were there. It wasn't because of my wealth, my status, my connections. We didn't meet at a charity gala, spotting each other across the room. She wasn't part of that fast life at all. Hers was slow, easy, real. The heaviness in my heart was both painful and bittersweet. The way I felt about this woman made me realize what I felt about Rose had never been real, even when our relationship was good. There wasn't this deep connection, this level of friendship, a relationship where the person wasn't just your lover, but your best friend.

She whispered back. "Goodnight, Dax..."

MY DRIVER PULLED up to the restaurant.

I looked at her in the seat beside me. "No reason to be nervous."

She turned to me, her eyebrow arched and high. "Nervous? Honey, I don't get nervous." She opened the door, flipped her hair, and stepped out of the car.

I grinned slightly before I joined her on the sidewalk. She was in a red dress, which looked lovely with her dark hair and fair complexion. The sleeves fell down her arms, and she wore black pumps. "I'm sorry we have to go to a fancy place. I've been told you hate pretentious food."

She grinned. "Don't worry about it. I know your sister and William like this sort of thing, so it's three to one. And now that I know there're two billionaires at the table, it doesn't bother me so much."

My arm circled her waist, and I pulled her close. "You look beautiful."

Her eyes softened at the compliment. "Thank you."

In truth, she looked incredible, sexy as hell, and I missed our alleyway fucks for a second.

"But you're the beautiful one."

That made me want to roll my eyes because no one noticed me when I stood beside her. My lips moved to hers, and I kissed her, careful not to ruin her red lipstick, but once our mouths were combined, the fire started.

I had to force myself to pull away and guide her into the restaurant. After I checked in at the desk, I was led to the table where Renee and William were already waiting. His arm was over the back of her chair, and he was pivoted toward her, giving his full attention to the woman who'd stolen his heart. He was in a sports jacket, and he was listening to her talk. Renee had her hair pulled back, and she was in a simple black dress.

Renee stopped talking when she saw us approach the table. "They're here."

William rose to his feet and shook my hand. "Long time, no see."

"Join us on Wednesday."

"I think I can make that happen." He turned to Carson next. "Wow...almost didn't recognize you. I'm used to seeing you in shorts with a basketball in your hands."

"And sweaty and gross," she added with a chuckle. "Yes, I look like a girl in real life."

"You look lovely." He embraced her with a one-armed hug. "And you look lovely on the court too."

She smiled at his compliment. "Thank you."

I moved to Renee next, giving her a brief hug. "You look nice."

"Thanks." She seemed to be the nervous one of the night, because she cleared her throat as she approached Carson. She extended her hand to shake hers. "It's nice to see you again. I hope we can get off on the right foot this time."

Carson didn't hesitate before she shook her hand. "There's no hard feelings, really. You were just protecting your own, and I respect that. And I've got rhino skin, so it's pretty much impossible to offend me. You've got to be that way in my line of work."

Renee nodded. "Well, I'm glad we can give this another go. And I'm very happy that you and my brother worked things out."

William turned to me. "What happened?"

I lowered my voice, so they wouldn't overhear. "Your woman came at Carson pretty hard when they met..."

"Ohh..." He nodded. "Yeah, the claws come out when she's mad."

"And thank you for the flowers," Carson said. "They're on my desk right now."

"Yes, Dax told me."

We took a seat at the table, where there was already a bottle of wine.

William passed it to me. "It's the vintage you ordered last time. Thought we could give it another round."

I poured a glass then poured hers.

Carson took a sip. "Not bad."

I returned the bottle to the table.

Renee sat across from Carson, and based on the way she tried to divert her gaze anywhere but at the person across the table, she was still uncomfortable with the whole thing. When she'd told off Carson, she must have thought there was no chance they would see each other again. It was the first time I'd seen Renee intimidated by another person.

It was another reason Carson had stolen my heart.

"Should we do an appetizer?" Carson grabbed the heavy menu. "I'm starving."

I smiled slightly. "Whatever you want, sweetheart."

"I'm hungry too." Renee looked at the menu. "What about the crab cakes?"

"Good choice." Carson turned to me. "Is that okay with you?"

I held her gaze. "Would it matter if it weren't?"

She suppressed her smile. "Just wanted to make sure."

"Crab cakes sound great," William said. "I'm not a picky eater."

"Neither am I," Carson said. "I just eat everything."

"It's true," I said. "Every time we get sandwiches, she eats her chips and then my chips..."

"Hey, I asked first," she said defensively. "Don't make me look like a chip hog."

The waitress came over, and we gave our order for the appetizer and the entrees.

My arm moved over the back of Carson's chair so my fingers could touch her shoulder lightly, feel her soft skin. We hadn't had another sleepover since our last one a few days ago, but it was the best night of sleep I'd gotten in a long time.

It was quiet for a while, like the awkwardness was still there.

William broke it. "Dax told me you played basketball in college. All four years?"

Carson nodded. "Yep."

"That's pretty impressive, especially since you went to Harvard," he said. "I heard they have a good team."

Carson turned her gaze on me, accusation in her eyes. "You told him?"

"Sweetheart, I'm proud that I'm dating a successful and intellectual woman." I knew I could defuse her anger with my charm because it'd always worked in the past. "It's hot. Can't blame me for wanting to brag."

"You should be proud," Renee said. "That's quite an accomplishment."

Carson's anger dimmed just like I thought it would. "I just don't like to brag about it. People usually assume I've got a stick up my ass..."

William chuckled at her crass comment. "Definitely don't have a stick up there, that's for sure."

"I get it," Renee said. "It's intimidating to most people, especially men you're trying to date."

"Except Dax." She grabbed her glass and took a drink. "He's not intimidated at all, which is one of the reasons I've come to adore him."

I turned back to her, staring at the side of her face, watching her drink from her glass again. My hand moved to her thigh under the table, my fingers immediately pulling up her dress slightly so I could get a sexy grip on her warm skin.

"He's so secure with himself and his masculinity that a woman's ambition doesn't affect his sense of worth. He's always been supportive of my career, always been interested in it, and my brash personality and candor seem intriguing to him rather than annoying. It's really nice to be with a man who's so…manly." She drank from her glass again, unapologetic about what she said in front of my sister.

Now I really stared at her, hanging on to the praise she never shared with me.

"He's not jealous either. I live with my best friend, who's a good-looking straight guy, and we work together at the newspaper. Most men just can't digest the relationship or approve of it, but Dax has never cared, accepted it from the beginning, because he's so secure that he doesn't get intimidated by other men either. Honestly, he's the perfect man." She spoke of me like I wasn't right beside her. "Why would he get jealous of other men when he's the best of his kind?"

She'd described me objectively, like I was a subject in an article, but those characteristics were the reason she came back to me, the reason she gave me another chance after I hurt her. I had always meant a lot to her, even though I hadn't realized that until now. She hadn't worn her heart on her sleeve in the past, but now that she did, she didn't hold anything back.

William shifted his gaze to me. "Safe to say…she's obsessed with you."

AFTER DINNER WAS FINISHED, we left the table and gathered on the sidewalk.

William skipped the handshake and embraced me with a hug and a pat on the back. "I'll be there on Wednesday. I've been craving hot wings anyway."

"So, do you actually want to play with us, or do you just want the food?"

He shrugged. "Mainly the food."

"You're a cardiologist, and you eat that shit?" I teased.

"Come on, you're gonna die anyway." He shrugged. "Do what you want, right?"

I turned to Renee. "You're welcome to play with us."

"Yeah," Carson said. "It would be nice to have another woman on the team."

"Oh no." Renee shook her head. "I can't even get myself on a treadmill."

"Running on a treadmill is totally different from a game," Carson said. "But if you don't want to play, you can still get dinner with us afterward."

"I'm more interested in that." Renee gave a thumbs-up.

"You can watch me play with my shirt off," William said. "We get all hot and sweaty."

Her reaction was immediately cold. "You take off your shirt?"

William's eyes widened like he'd been caught doing something he shouldn't. He turned his gaze back to me. "What did I tell you? My baby gets jealous, *really* jealous."

"I'm not jealous," she argued. "I just don't want you playing half naked while a bunch of women stare at you."

William wrapped his arm around her waist and started to guide her away. "You guys have a good night. I've got to get yelled at for twenty minutes."

I watched them walk away, their voices growing inaudible as Renee continued to talk his ear off.

"They're cute." Carson stood beside me, her arms crossed over her chest. "They go well together."

My arm moved around her waist, and I tugged her close. "We're cute."

Her arm slipped around my waist, and she looked up at me. "I don't know… I'm not the jealous type."

"I have a feeling that's going to change." My hand gripped her ass in her dress as I kissed her, my dick impossible to control in my slacks. My pants suddenly became very tight, but when she wore a red dress like that and talked about me like I was God's gift to women, it was impossible not to lose my mind. I ended the kiss but kept our faces close. "Based on all those things you said about me."

Her hands slid up my chest as she arched her back, pressing her body farther into mine, her lips slightly parted, her eyes both hot and playful. "They were just compliments..."

"No, they weren't." I squeezed her ass again. "You love it when I grab you like this because every woman in sight knows that I'm yours, that the only woman who's getting my dick is you." My lips moved to hers, and I gave her a small kiss. "You took me back because I'm the only man you want. You don't trust yourself around me because you want me so much. We both know you're ready, but you're taking your time crossing the line, because once you do...everything will be different. Trust me, if a woman looks at me too long, it'll drive you fucking crazy." I kissed her again. "And I want it to."

EIGHTEEN

CARSON

After I got off work, I went by Kat's apartment.

We hadn't spoken in a week, and since we were going out on Friday night, I thought I should see where she was at. Emotionally.

She opened the door with a slight look of surprise, as if she hadn't expected to hear from me.

I held up the box of muffins. "I got the last two poppy seed muffins."

Her eyes moved to the box before she stepped aside and let me enter. "Both for me, right?"

I chuckled. "Girl, I'm not that nice." I placed the box on the counter and handed one to her before I peeled back the paper on my own and took a bite.

She stood across from me at the kitchen island as she took a few bites. "I've eaten so much this week, but I don't even care."

"Not feeling better?"

"I mean, I'm better now than I was last week…"

I set the muffin on a napkin. "I'm sorry."

"Yeah, me too. The sex with Nathan is great, but not great enough."

"In my experience, sex isn't going to fix your problems. Trust me…I know."

"Yeah." She gave me a sympathetic look. "Have you slept with him yet?"

"I don't want to talk about him. I want to talk about you." I hadn't thought I could be happy again, but Dax was really making me happy. Or maybe he wasn't doing anything—I was just allowing myself to feel good. My heart was open, and I let everything spill out every day. I also absorbed everything he gave, right into my bloodstream. Talking about how I'd overcome my problems and possibly found the guy I wanted to spend my life seemed cruel, considering her pain. "Is there anything I can do to help?"

She shook her head. "No. I just need to move on…" She set her muffin down, half eaten. "Over the course of this week, I've come to realize how pathetic I am. When Charlie dumped me, I should have toughened up and moved on. I shouldn't have waited around and pined for a man who doesn't even want me. Embarrassing…"

"Kat, it's not embarrassing," I said gently. "We all handle heartbreak differently. Nothing to be ashamed of. Look at me."

"But you were married. It's totally different."

"You and Charlie were together as long as I was married. Not much different to me."

She leaned against the counter and crossed her arms over her chest.

"Does this affect your friendship with Charlie and Denise?"

She shrugged. "Not sure. I mean, nothing has happened, so it's not like I can get mad at them. Technically, Charlie doesn't owe me anything."

"He values his friendship with you a lot, Kat."

"He said that?" she whispered.

"Of course. He values the entire group. We're all a family, you know? And Denise said she couldn't betray you either. Their loyalty is in the right place. If you never wanted anything to happen, it wouldn't. But...I think that would be wrong."

She stared at me, her eyes losing their light. "You think I should step aside?"

"I didn't say that."

"But you're implying it."

Now I was backed into a corner. "I know this is hard for you, it would be hard for anybody, but if these two people want to be together...I think you should let it happen. Maybe not right this second, but at some point."

She sighed. "Denise is gorgeous and can have anyone she wants, and Charlie can get any piece of ass he wants. Why do they necessarily have to be together, so I have to look at it all the time? They can just find someone else."

"What's the difference between Charlie being with Denise or being with someone else? Either way, you're going to see him with another woman. He's going to bring her over for games or when we go out."

"Yes, but she's my friend. I'll have to hear all about how she feels about him."

"She would never do that, Kat."

"It's still weird. She knows I'm still in love with him. I feel like the loser Charlie didn't want…"

That was a little too close for comfort. "You aren't a loser, Kat. Life just happens, and sometimes it's not fair and it doesn't make sense—but it happens whether you want it to or not. As hard as it is, I think the best thing for you to do is handle this with dignity. Hold your head high and be the bigger person."

She rolled her eyes. "Would you be able to hold your head high? If the woman Evan left you for was your friend?"

"Not the same thing at all."

"I just know if you were in this situation, you wouldn't be so inclined to accept it."

"No. It would suck. But…I would do it."

She looked away.

"Kat."

She wouldn't look at me.

"It will get easier. I promise."

She shook her head, her arms across her chest. "Why are you pushing for this so hard? Are they in love with each other or something? Is there something you aren't telling me?"

I felt terrible lying, but I had to lie so she wouldn't be crushed. "I just feel torn because Charlie is my best friend and Denise is my sister. It feels like a disservice to them both to just look the other way."

"But there are rules for this, you know? Don't date your friend's ex. Don't date the ex your friend is still in love with. Don't date your best friend's sister, who's a friend of your ex. I mean, this is just so obvious."

"I know, but you've been broken up for almost a year."

She sighed again. "If I were over him, I guess that would be a valid argument, but I'm not."

"Yeah..."

She straightened and grabbed the muffin again and started to pick at it. The conversation seemed to be over, based on the way she kept her gaze averted as she ate.

"We were going to out on Friday. You want to come?"

"Everyone?"

I nodded.

"Yeah...that's fine. You guys mean a lot to me, and I don't want to lose you because of this."

"You could never lose us, Kat." Unless she was the one to walk away.

"Alright, so tell me what's going on with Dax."

"JUST FUCK HIM ALREADY." Matt walked beside me as we headed to the gym to play our weekly sport. "Do you have any idea how hot he is? How do you restrain yourself when he smiles like that?"

"Trust me, I know. I've already fucked him."

"Then it's even more shocking that you're holding back."

"It'll happen when it's meant to happen."

"How long has it been?"

"Couple weeks."

He shook his head. "The guy is a saint. So, what's going on with Kat?"

I shook my head. "Haven't gotten anywhere with her, but she's coming out with us on Friday night."

"They've been broken up a long time. She should be over it."

"Don't be a dick, Matt."

"What?" he asked incredulously.

"You don't know what it's like to be in love and then get dumped."

"True. But how are you going to change her mind?"

I started to wonder if the only option was to tell her the truth…that Charlie ended their relationship because Denise was the one he really wanted. It would explain why she needed to let this happen, but it would also kill her. "Not sure."

We entered the gym and saw Charlie there—with Denise.

They sat together on the bench, talking while the guys warmed up on the court. He was shirtless and drinking from his water bottle. She was in skintight black jeans with brown booties and a sweater, her hair in curls down her chest, bracelets on her wrist.

"Hopefully, Kat gets on board soon," Matt said. "Because it looks like it might happen whether she's ready or not."

I didn't even look at the court because I was more focused on the two of them, close together and engaged in conversation. He said something to make her laugh, and she touched his arm, which seemed innocent, but since I was aware of her attraction, I knew it was anything but.

I took a seat beside Charlie on the bench. "Ready for this?"

He turned to me, a guilty look in his eyes like he knew what I was really thinking. We were connected like that, so it was easy to read his mind. "Yeah."

"I didn't know you were coming." I leaned forward and looked at Denise.

"Charlie invited me," Denise said. "Since there's pizza and beer afterward, I couldn't say no. Plus, all the hot shirtless guys on the court."

"That better not include Dax."

Denise smiled. "Sis, he's all yours."

Dax had walked up and embraced Charlie. After Charlie jogged onto the court, Dax stood over me. "Get your ass up, sweetheart."

I recognized the playfulness in his tone, but also the subtle offense because I hadn't gone out of my way to greet him like I usually did. I set my stuff down and got to my feet, having to tilt my chin back to look at him. "Hey…" The second I looked into his face, I forgot about the dilemma playing out right in front of me. My hands moved around his waist, and I rose onto my tiptoes to kiss him.

His powerful arms tugged me against his hard body, and he kissed me hard, as if he didn't care that my sister was right there. Like always, his hand snaked to my ass and gave one cheek a tight squeeze. "That's better." He pulled away and brushed his nose against mine. "What did I tell you?"

I cocked an eyebrow, not following his question.

He grinned, arrogance in his eyes. "I heard what you said, sweetheart. Would you like me to keep my shirt on?"

I rolled my eyes and gave a good-natured shove into his chest so I could walk away and onto the court.

He grabbed me by the wrist and tugged me back, his hand capturing my ponytail and forcing my head back so he could press another kiss to my mouth, this one even more aggressive than the last.

Then he abruptly released me, walking back on the court like nothing happened.

I turned back to Denise.

Denise fanned herself and mouthed, "Damn."

I jogged onto the court, and we started the game.

Dax was on me like usual, touching me in so many ways that were illegal during a real game. Even when I didn't have the ball, his hands were on my hips or on my ass. He pressed his naked chest and stomach into my body, his face coming close like he would kiss me if the right opening occurred.

"Geez, you're ridiculous." I gave him a playful shove in the chest.

"Sweetheart, you like it." He grabbed my wrists and planted them on his sweat-soaked body.

I shoved him and sprinted off, trying to get open to grab the ball. It was the perfect moment, because I caught the pass and dribbled across the court and reached the basket. I made the shot, using the backboard to sink the two-pointer.

Dax stood with his hands on his hips, grinning at me even though I'd gotten away.

Charlie got the ball and started to dribble as he prepared to pass to someone.

I stayed close with my hands open. "What the fuck are you doing?"

"What the fuck are *you* doing?" he snapped. "Get open."

Dax was on me now, covering me and finding any reason to touch me.

I pushed him aside and stuck out my head. "Why the hell did you invite Denise here?"

Once Dax realized I was just trying to talk to Charlie, he eased up on the blocking.

Charlie sighed. "We're playing a game here."

"Don't be a dick, Charlie," I snapped.

"I'm not," he snapped back. "She texted me the day before about something, so I just decided to invite her. It's not like I asked her out on a date or something. We're friends, right?"

"But you know your intentions aren't friendly."

The guys started to shout from the other end of the court.

Dax started to block me more seriously to make this believable. "You guys are going to have to talk about this later."

"Oh, we will," I snapped. Then I took off, running down the court and trying to leave Dax behind me.

He was too fast and caught up to me, blocking me in the corner. "I know you're trying to keep everyone happy, but I'm not sure if you can."

"Well, I'm going to try."

WILLIAM WIPED down with a towel as he sat on the bench. "We need to mix up the teams, because Charlie and Carson can communicate telepathically or something."

Charlie stood close to Denise and wiped down with his towel, starting with his face and then his body.

She stared.

I did not want this to happen now. I wanted this to happen when the moment was right. Charlie clearly had grown impatient waiting, and when Kat didn't give the green light, he snapped. He'd been waiting long enough and couldn't do it for several more months, however long Kat needed.

"What are we eating?" Matt asked.

"I've been craving hot wings," William said.

"Me too," Denise said. "Even though I didn't work up a sweat at all."

We filed out of the gym and headed down the sidewalk.

Dax was beside me, drawing the attention of each woman who passed. Being sweaty made him look even better, so he turned every single head.

It didn't bother me, despite what he claimed, because they couldn't have him.

I watched Charlie, Matt, and Denise walk up ahead. Thankfully, Matt was there, so it wouldn't be too much one-on-one time.

Dax glanced at me. "It's out of your control."

"I just need to give Charlie a reminder when we're alone together." And I would give him a big-ass reminder.

William was on the other side of Dax. "Renee almost came today, but she bailed at the last minute. Had to do something at the office."

"You kept your shirt on," Dax noted.

"Because if she found out..." He shook his head and whistled. "She'd burn the gym down with her fire. She acts all professional around other people, but with me, she's an emotional wreck. I love it." He grinned.

"My woman is like that too." Dax gave me a teasing stare.

"Am not," I argued.

"That's not what it sounded like when you spoke to your sister," Dax noted.

"I was teasing," I said.

"Sure..." He gave me a gentle tickle in the side. "Whatever you say."

"I don't have to put up with this." I walked ahead and came to the other side of Dense.

She turned to me. "You were on fire on the court today."

"Thanks." I was glad she looked at me and didn't stare at Charlie the entire time. "What's new with you?" Without turning around, I could feel Dax's gaze right on my ass. I glanced over my shoulder to see him doing exactly that.

When he knew I checked, he grinned—unapologetically.

"I just finished my rotation," she said. "I'm off for four days."

"Cool. Any plans?"

"Not really. I have a date on Saturday, but I don't know if I'm gonna go."

Charlie ended his conversation with Matt abruptly and turned in her direction when he heard what she said.

"Why not?" I asked.

She shrugged. "I just think I'm not going to like him, so I don't want to waste his time. He's a neurologist."

"Do you only date doctors?" I asked incredulously.

"No," she said with a laugh. "But I see them a lot, and it kinda just happens."

Charlie turned away and continued his conversation with Matt, but his tone was definitely different.

We entered the restaurant and took up a large table. I made sure to say near Denise and Charlie to interrupt anything inappropriate, and Dax sat on the other side of me, his hand moving to my thigh under the table.

I kept Denise engaged so she wouldn't pay much attention to Charlie.

Charlie glared at me because I was being the biggest cockblock on the planet.

The food arrived and everyone ate, washing it down with their beers. Dax talked to William because I was so focused on the drama unfolding right in front of me.

Dax moved his arm around my chair and leaned in close to kiss me. "Sweetheart?"

"Hmm?"

"I'd like some attention too."

I lowered my voice. "I've got to cockblock this thing."

"You're pretty small. Not sure you could block Charlie's cock."

"Well, I have to try. I'm not gonna let this take off and then Kat finds out, and it's just terrible…"

His hand moved to my back, and he rubbed me gently, the playfulness leaving his gaze and being replaced by a softer look. "It's sweet that you're so invested in other people's feelings, but there's nothing you can do. If it's going to happen, it's going to happen. And it's not your fault."

I propped my chin on my knuckles and sighed.

He pulled me in and kissed the corner of my mouth, the stubble on his jaw scratching my soft skin lightly. "It'll be alright, sweetheart."

ONCE WE LEFT the restaurant and said goodbye, I grilled Charlie—hard. "What are you doing right now?"

"Walking," he said, like a smartass.

"I'm serious."

He shook his head and kept walking, crossing the street with me in tow. "I just invited her to watch the game. You're making this a much bigger deal than it needs to be."

"Charlie."

He ignored me.

"Charlie." I grabbed his arm and forced him to halt.

He turned to me, his jaw clenched.

"You know exactly what you're doing."

"How would you feel if the woman you've wanted forever wants you too? I just do nothing? You know how impossible that is?"

"I know, I get it."

"No, you don't get it," he snapped. "I'm sorry Kat feels the way she does. Truly, I am. But I'm not going to not be happy just because she isn't. This is what I want. I'm tired of living for someone else's feelings instead of my own."

"I get it." I raised both hands to calm him down.

"And we're great together. I make her laugh, she makes me laugh, we're connecting. I've never really connected with her before because there's been this fucking wall between us since I can't do anything. But now that I know she feels the way I do…I can't help it. I flirt. I smile. I compliment her. And if I don't continue to do that, she's gonna end up with some other guy, and that's the worst thing that can happen."

"Just give it a little more time."

His hands moved to his hips, and he glared at me. "It's been nine months—"

"Just a little more time."

"Then I get to talk to Denise and tell her I want to ask her out, but I'm waiting for Kat's fucking permission."

"We can't do that."

"Why the hell not?"

"Because then you really are sneaking around behind her back."

He pressed his palms over his eyes then slowly dragged them down. "You're killing me here, Carson. She's gonna go out with that neurologist unless I step up."

"She said she's probably gonna cancel that."

"And then some other guy will ask her out. She's fucking gorgeous, Carson. I'm surprised she's been single as long as she has."

"Chill." I lowered my hands.

His nostrils flared. "You've talked to Kat twice, and she hasn't come around. And honestly, if she doesn't come around, it's not going to stop me. I've tried to do the right thing and be as sensitive as possible, but I'm getting tired... really tired."

I wasn't sure if Kat would ever be on board. She was making some progress, but not enough. "If it really comes down to it, I know one thing that will get her on board...but I don't want to take that option."

"What is it?"

"We tell her the real reason you ended things."

His eyes shifted back and forth as he looked into mine.

"Because she doesn't understand why you can't just find someone else and Denise can't find someone else. There are a million women out there, and it doesn't need to be Denise. So if I tell her the reason why this is so important to you, she would definitely bow out...but be eternally heartbroken."

He sighed, like his lungs ached. "Yeah...I don't want to do that."

"I don't either. But it might come down to it."

"That's just cruel, Carson."

"I know. But if there's no other way..."

"If it comes down to it, then she should hear it from me."

"I don't know. That might make it worse."

"But if you tell her, then she'll know you knew the whole time. And that will put you in a really tough position."

"I know, but it'll still hurt a lot less."

NINETEEN
CARSON

Charlie and I were the first ones there.

He got me a lemon drop and grabbed himself a beer. We stood at the table together, him dressed in jeans and a t-shirt, me in a black dress that had slits in the material, showing the side of my stomach and my upper thigh. My hair was pulled back slightly, the curls pinned in an elegant updo. A lot of the guys stared at me but didn't make a pass because they assumed I was with Charlie.

Charlie was totally immune to my looks. He never showed a hint of attraction for me, looked at me like I was the little sister he both loved and hated. Our personalities meshed together so well that we'd felt like family the moment we met, but that romantic connection, like what I felt with Dax, had never been there. Sometimes people said Charlie and I would be perfect together, but those urges weren't present...for either of us.

"Fuck." Charlie straightened and bought his beer to his lips, his eyes on the door.

"What?" I turned to see Denise walk inside in a deep green dress with one sleeve, her curled hair down one shoulder with her clutch hanging from her wrist on a string. Her makeup was fully done, and there wasn't a guy in that bar who didn't notice her the way Charlie did.

Charlie quickly stuck his fist into his mouth and bit down, like he needed to express his frustration in some way. He dropped his hand and straightened. "Fuck. Fuck. Fuck."

"Keep it together, man." I nudged him in the side.

He sighed and tried to look casual.

Denise noticed us and came to our table, a smile spreading on her lips when she reached us. "Hey." She hugged me. "You look hot. Trying to give Dax a heart attack?"

"You're the one giving people a heart attack…" If only she knew how much.

She turned to Charlie next, her smile growing, her eyes wearing a special shine. "Hey."

"Hey." He hesitated for a brief second before he wrapped his arm around her and hugged her to his chest, his fingers spread out over her back, his eyes closed as he held her. When he released her, he took his time letting go, his hand sliding over her back and to her hip before he finally dropped his embrace. "Can I get you something to drink?"

"Sure. Surprise me."

"Be right back." He walked away and headed to the bar.

Denise turned back to me as if nothing happened.

"Now I know the real reason you canceled that date with the neurologist." I brought the glass to my lips and took a drink.

Denise rolled her eyes. "Coincidence."

"Girl, you're so full of shit."

She shrugged. "Charlie is so hot. How have you guys never hooked up?"

"Because there's zero attraction," I said. "Seriously."

"Seriously?" she asked incredulously. "He's gorgeous."

"Eh." I shrugged. "I disagree. Now, Dax...he's gorgeous."

"Well, of course he is," she said. "But so is Charlie."

"It's never happened, and it never will happen."

"That's amazing," she said. "I've never had a guy friend who wasn't gay."

Charlie returned a moment later, getting her a lemon drop. He stepped away from her and pivoted his body, facing her completely, ignoring everyone else in the room—including me. "How was your day?"

"I slept in since I was off, so it was amazing." She grabbed her glass and took a drink. "And thanks for this."

I stood on the other side of the table, basically a loner because they had obviously paired off. I hoped Kat wouldn't read too much into it when she walked inside.

Dax entered a moment later, and the only reason I knew that was because the women in my vicinity all turned to the entryway like someone famous had just walked inside. I turned to look at him, seeing him push through the crowd in black jeans and a gray t-shirt. His sexy stubble was on his jawline, and his short hair was styled. His eyes scanned the bar, ignoring the attention cast on him, and stopped when he saw me.

I gave him a gentle wave with my fingers.

He stood there for a second, his eyes roaming over my appearance in the tight black dress. They moved all the way down, to my feet in my pumps. When he raised his gaze to look at my face once more, his chest rose visibly, like he needed to take a breath before he continued toward me.

A man had never made me feel so sexy just by looking at me.

He approached the table, his arm circling my waist as he bent his head down to kiss my lips, to seal his mouth over mine and take a deep breath when he felt the spark. His hand groped my ass like always, and he kissed me harder, just as he did last time we were here. Then his lips moved to my ear, where he breathed hard. "Jesus fucking Christ." His hand squeezed my ass hard before he walked away and headed to the bar to get himself a drink.

Charlie and Denise were both staring at me.

"What?" I asked, feeling the burn in my throat.

"Give it up already," Denise said. "How the hell are your thighs still closed?"

Charlie chuckled at her crass comment.

I rolled my eyes and brought my drink to my lips. My eyes shifted to the bar so I could admire him, seeing the way his shoulders and arms stretched his t-shirt, see the way his brown eyes looked bright from all the way across the room.

He stood at the bar, ordered his drink with his one arm resting on the surface, and then a sexy little thang came over to talk to him.

Not gonna happen, biotch.

But Dax turned to her, smiled, and gave her a hug. Then he stayed at the bar and talked to her. She was a small brunette with long curled hair, and her deep blue dress was nice against her skin tone.

"Ooh...she's trying to take your man." Matt appeared at my side.

"No, she's not," I said. "They obviously know each other." I turned away so I wouldn't continue to stare.

Matt kept his eyes on the drama. "The only women Dax knows are women he's slept with."

Now my heart dropped into my stomach, so I took a drink from my glass.

Charlie stared at me, standing closer to Denise than he should. "Look at her, she's losing her mind."

"I am not," I said calmly.

"You're totally jealous," Charlie said. "Your face is getting all red, you're flustered..."

"I don't get jealous," I snapped. "Did you see the way he just kissed me and grabbed my ass?"

"And he's probably done the same to her," Matt said, his eyes still on Dax. "They're still talking..."

I turned to him, getting a little angry. "Why are you trying to get a rise out of me?"

"I'm not," Matt said. "I just think he's hot, so I like to stare, and he happens to be talking to an equally hot woman... That's all."

Charlie set his beer down. "You're jealous. Just admit it."

"I'm not," I said calmly. "You guys are just trying to make this into a dramatic situation." I drank from my lemon drop again, making it empty.

"I've never seen you drink a lemon drop that quickly," Denise said. "So—"

"He's coming back," Matt said.

"Everyone just shut up and don't say anything," I said. "I'm not going to be one of those obnoxious people who gets jealous every time her man is talking to a woman. I'm too secure for that. Too classy for that."

"Whatever you say." Charlie drank from his beer.

Dax came back to the table, a glass of scotch in hand.

We were all quiet...suspiciously quiet.

His arm moved around my waist, and he took a drink.

My temper flared out of nowhere. "Did you grab her ass?"

He almost had to spit it out because the question caught him off guard. He wiped the drops from his lips with the back of his forearm then he looked down at me, his eyes filled with surprise.

Matt rested his forehead on the table and laughed uncontrollably, trying to mute it against the wood.

Charlie grinned. "Smooth..."

Denise covered her mouth and tried not to laugh too hard.

"Grab whose ass?" Dax set down his glass and turned to me.

"That woman you were talking to." I couldn't think rationally at all, because I kept picturing him kissing her and grabbing her ass the way he grabbed mine every time he saw me.

"No...I didn't grab her ass." He glanced at everyone at the table, seeing them all laughing. "Am I missing something here?"

"I don't mean right *now*," I snapped. "But when you were together."

"Why do you assume we were together?" he asked, his eyebrows furrowed.

"Because she's hot." I looked into his face, the jealousy running rampant like a wild animal that had just escaped a cage.

Once Dax understood the situation, that arrogant smile started to stretch over his lips, like this was absolutely hilarious. He leaned his elbow on the table and looked at me, his eyes more playful than they'd ever been. "Damn...you're so fucking hot when you're jealous."

"I'm not jealous—"

"You're seriously going to look me in the eye and say that?" His sexy grin was obnoxious right now because he was enjoying this far too much. "Sweetheart, it looks like your head is about to explode."

I turned away to storm off.

He grabbed me by the wrist and yanked me back. "Nothing to be embarrassed about. It's hot... I love it." His arms circled me and held me close to his body.

"You never answered my question."

"What?"

"Did you grab her ass?"

He released me, still smiling. "I'm sorry, this is a weird question. Can I have some backstory?"

Charlie stuck himself in the conversation. "At first, she tried to pretend she wasn't jealous, even though she clearly was. But she also said there was nothing to be jealous about because of the way you'd just kissed her and groped her ass."

Dax kept his eyes on me and gave a slight nod in agreement.

"But then Matt said you've probably grabbed her ass too," Charlie said. "I think that's what made her snap."

Dax's eyes darkened as his hand went to my cheek. "Now I get it, sweetheart. I knew you loved it when I grabbed your ass, but I had no idea how much." His fingers slid to my neck, and he brought me close, held me like we were lovers when he hadn't been between my legs in months. "No is my answer. Is that better?" His thumb slid across my jawline, his eyes looking at my lips. "Hmm?"

"A bit…"

"Would it also help to know your ass is the only ass I want to squeeze…ever."

Charlie and Denise both made an aww noise.

Matt straightened and grinned. "Smooth, man."

"How's that?" he whispered.

I gave a slight nod before I turned my lips into his palm and kissed his hand.

His gaze intensified.

I moved into his chest and rested my forehead against his chest.

His arms circled around me, and he placed a kiss to my forehead. "I can't wait to make love to you."

I closed my eyes and held him close, never wanting to let him go, never wanting to share. Once I opened my heart, he infected me, entered every part of my body until he had complete control over me. I was emotional, delirious...even crazy. I had fallen so deeply, fallen so hard, that it made me wonder if I'd ever loved Evan...because I'd never felt this way. "Me too."

KAT WALKED INSIDE and headed to our table.

"Hey, girl." I tried to be overly bubbly for her, to make this night go as smoothly as possible. "Damn, you look hot."

She smiled, but it didn't reach her eyes. "Thanks..." Her eyes shifted to Charlie and Denise.

They were so absorbed in their conversation, the music so loud, that they didn't even notice Kat approach. And Charlie was staring at Denise with that look...the kind of look that Dax gave to me.

I purposely knocked over my drink to get their attention.

"Whoa, had too much to drink, Carson?" Charlie grabbed the napkins and threw them on the liquor that spread across the table.

"Maybe." I threw my napkin on top to stop the spread.

"I'm going to get more napkins." Denise headed to the bar.

Charlie obviously had no idea Kat was there because he turned to watch her go, to stare at her ass.

Ugh, why was this happening right now?

Dax tried to help. "Charlie, did you see the game last night?"

Charlie turned back to him and kept dampening the napkins with the booze. "Yeah. The last play of the game…"

I turned to Kat, hoping she hadn't noticed, but it was obvious she had.

Because she looked like she was about to cry.

WHEN KAT WENT to the bathroom, I was on Charlie. "Seriously, knock it off."

"What?" he asked, genuinely bewildered.

"She saw you stare at Denise's ass, and she's probably crying in the bathroom right now."

"I stare at a lot of women's asses. Doesn't mean anything."

"But she knows you have feelings for Denise, so it's totally different. Charlie, I'm going to bitch-slap you if you don't get your shit together. You're being a selfish pig right now."

"Whoa, sweetheart." Dax came up behind me and wrapped his arm around my stomach, pulling me back a little bit. "Let's take it down a notch."

"I can't stop you from seeing Denise in private, but you knew Kat was coming tonight," I said.

"I didn't know she was here. And if everything I do is going to be dissected, then I can't hide it from her anyway." He threw his arms up in the air. "I can't hide the way I looked at Denise. I can't hide the way I talk to her. I've *always* looked at Denise this way. Kat is just noticing now. The only way I can truly keep myself in check is if I don't see Denise at all when Kat's around."

"Well, maybe that's what we need to do for a bit."

Charlie shook his head. "I'm not a selfish pig. I'm a man with emotions, emotions that I can't hide. That's like me telling you not to act like you're head over heels for Dax. You can't control it. It's fucking impossible. If I didn't stare at Denise's ass, Kat would have noticed something else I did."

I knew he was right, so I calmed down. "I'm sorry..."

He looked away, still angry.

Dax remained beside us, his arm still around me. "I think Carson is coming on a little strong right now because she wants everyone to be happy, for no one to get hurt. She wants you to be happy. Otherwise, she wouldn't have talked to Kat for you in the first place. So, she's in your corner, man. But she's trying to protect her friend too."

Charlie turned back to me, less angry than he was before.

I appreciated that Dax intervened, that he wanted to keep us close and dissolve our fights because he knew how important this relationship was to me. Charlie was my best friend, and Dax fully supported that.

Charlie finally nodded. "It's okay."

I moved my hand to his arm and gave him a gentle squeeze. "I should go talk to Kat now…" I left the guys behind and went to the bathroom. There was a long line of girls, and Kat was nowhere in sight. "A crying girl come through here?"

One woman nodded to the closed door. "We let her go first because it looked like she needed it."

I banged my fists on the door. "Kat, open up." If she said something on the other side, I couldn't hear it because the music was too loud. I knocked again and turned to the girl at the front of the line. "Her ex that she's still in love is hung up on her friend, and she just found out and she's just upset."

She shook her head. "Been there…"

Kat opened the door, her makeup ruined.

"Girl…" I shut the door behind me then hugged her.

She held on to me tightly, the music thudding loudly outside.

I rubbed her back. "I know it hurts… I know."

She pulled away, new tears in her eyes. "It's just… I can't even describe it."

"I know." I rubbed her arms, comforting her.

"I don't think I can do this. Even without them being together, just seeing him look at her the way he used to look at me... It's too much."

"Kat, don't say that."

"Not forever. Just for a while..."

"No. We're all friends here. We don't want you to take a step back." It was the very thing I'd feared would happen. I didn't want to lose my best friend, for us to talk less and less until she moved on and found a new life.

"I know, but it's just too hard. What does she have that I don't?"

"Nothing, Kat. It's just how life is sometimes."

"The fact that he won't just find someone else makes me sick. He's so selfish..."

I dropped my gaze, wondering if I should just tell her now, rip off all the bandages in one go. "He's not selfish, Kat. If you wanted to be with Matt or something, even if it made him uncomfortable, he wouldn't let it affect your friendship."

"Easy to say when I'm the one in love and he's not."

"But I know him, Kat," I said. "If the situations were reversed, he would do it in a heartbeat."

She stepped back and crossed her arms over her chest. "Either way, I can't go back out there now. I should get home."

I couldn't ask her to stay, not when her eyes were red and puffy. "I'll walk you."

"Alright. Thanks."

We left the bathroom and headed to the door. I didn't stop at the table so everyone would see her, which meant I couldn't tell Dax where I was going. I'd text him whenever I had a chance.

We made it to the sidewalk.

"Carson."

I turned at the sound of Dax's voice. Apparently, his eyes were always on me, even when I had no idea. "I'm going to take Kat home."

Kat walked off to the curb of the sidewalk, hiding her face so Dax wouldn't see.

"She's not…feeling well," I said.

Dax pulled out his phone and texted someone.

I raised an eyebrow at his actions, wondering what was so important right this second.

He returned the phone to his pocket. "My driver will take you."

"What?" I asked, seeing a black car pull up immediately. "Dax, we don't—"

"You've accepted me. Please accept my wealth too." His arms circled my waist, and he moved his head to mine, giving me an embrace more intimate than sex. "Rich or poor, I want to take care of you." His hand cupped my cheek, and he closed his eyes as he held me, like nothing else in the world mattered except the two of us.

I could feel a powerful sensation everywhere, an emotional pull that made me so happy I was delirious. I would normally reject his offer or at least argue with it, but I didn't want to. "Okay..."

He cupped my face and kissed me. "I'm going to head home. If you want to join me afterward, I'll be there."

"You aren't going to go back inside?"

"There's no reason for me to be there without you. My bar days are over."

TWENTY
CARSON

I stayed with Kat for a few hours before I got back in the car.

When the driver asked where I wanted to go, I knew what my answer should be. But instead of doing what I should do, I did what I wanted to do.

I went to Dax's penthouse.

I checked in with the security officer inside then rose in the elevator to his gorgeous penthouse that was thousands of feet too big for a single person. The windows were lit up with the lights from the skyscrapers in the background, the bridge in the distance. A few lamps were on, and he had dimmer lights that gave the living room a romantic ambiance. It was cozy, a place easy to get comfortable in.

Dax was on the couch in his sweatpants, as if he'd known I would come. The *New York Press* was on the table.

The article about him had been published that morning. I'd totally forgotten about it.

He rose, his muscular arms extending from his broad shoulders, his tight stomach flat like a straight line. The alcohol didn't make his stomach stick out like it did for me. He walked to me, his eyes looking into my face, reading every subtle expression like he knew me better than Charlie.

When he reached me, his hands dug into my hair, ignoring the pins that kept it in place, and he gave me a kiss that was both passionate and comforting. His full lips moved with mine, conveying his concern as well as his affection. When he ended the kiss, his hands slid down my shoulders and arms until his hands squeezed mine. He looked at me and asked a question with his eyes instead of his lips.

"She was upset at first but calmed down after a while…"

"It's unfortunate, but maybe it's a good thing. She's seen it with her own eyes, so she'll be prepared."

"Yeah, maybe…" My hands gravitated to his chest, feeling the solid concrete that could protect me from anything. His skin was warm to the touch, and with his shirt gone, I could really smell his cologne. "Thanks for mediating between Charlie and me…"

"Just wanted him to remember how much you care about him…since he's your best friend." He stepped into me and pressed a kiss to my forehead, his lips light a hot pan that seared my skin.

I loved having a man who was so secure that he didn't care that my roommate was a man. I loved having a man who would fight for my relationships instead of ripping them apart. I loved having a man who went out of his way to be friends with my friends without even being asked.

"You want to sleep over?" His lips brushed against my skin as he spoke.

I nodded.

He turned away and closed up the penthouse, turning off the lamps and the TV. His drink was left on the table to be addressed tomorrow. He stopped at the entrance to his hallway and turned around to look at me.

I'd never been in his bedroom before. I'd just realized it for the first time.

He stared for a few seconds before he moved down the hallway.

I watched him go before I followed, entering the master bedroom at the end of the hallway. It was a large room with very little inside. It was a corner bedroom, so two of the walls were just windows, overlooking the city. There was no TV across from his bed. It was against the other wall, on an arm that could push the TV out and turn it if he wanted to watch it. A large dresser was underneath it, along with two paintings on either side of the TV. He had a nightstand on each side of the bed and a dark wooden headboard. Above it was a painting of a dark landscape, a jagged mountain with masculine colors and tones.

"You can use my toothbrush if you want." He set his phone on his nightstand and dropped his sweatpants before he pulled back the covers and got inside, lying on his back with his hand behind his head. The sheets reached his waist, showing all his hardness above.

I stared at him in the bed and came closer, my heels moving to the rug around his bed.

"There're shirts in my dresser."

There was a bench at the end of the bed, so I sat down and got my heels off, undoing the straps over my feet so they could slide off and tip over onto the rug. When I stood up, I faced the Manhattan lights outside the window, the quietness of a loud city. My hand reached behind my back and found the zipper there. I pinched it between my fingers and slowly pulled it down, letting the material come off my body until it was loose enough that I could pull it over my hips and let it slide the rest of the way to the ground.

The breath Dax took was audible.

I reached behind me and unclasped the black bra. It came loose, and I pulled the straps down. The last thing was the matching thong I wore, so I bent and pushed it over my hips until it slid down my legs to my ankles. I stepped out of it and turned around.

Dax was up against the headboard, a whole new look of intensity I'd never seen before on his face. His dark eyes were on me, and his chest rose and fell at a quicker rate, like his excitement alone made his blood desperate for more oxygen.

My eyes remained on his, watching him visibly desire me, do his best not to drop his gaze and look at my tits, stomach, and the perfectly groomed area between my legs. I pulled the sheets back then crawled into the bed, moving closer to him until our faces were practically touching.

His hand snaked into my hair, but he didn't kiss me.

I pushed the covers down so I could tug on his boxers, get them over his hips a little, until the top of his hard dick emerged. My intentions were perfectly clear—this was what I wanted; I didn't want to wait another night...not when I was ready.

He pushed his boxers down before his hand dug into my hair, ignoring the pins and tugging them free as he kissed me. It was a slow kiss, a gentle beginning, and he breathed directly into my mouth once the kiss grew stronger, deeper, more passionate.

He rolled me onto my back, his body moving with mine, his knees separating my thighs as his kiss remained just as intense as before. His mass sank me into his mattress and sheets, and once his cock was pressed against me, it felt like an iron rod with heat running through it.

His lips moved down my neck, over my collarbone, and he secured his hand tightly in my hair to keep my head pinned to the pillow. His tongue glided down, and he kissed both of my breasts, handling my hard nipples with masculine gentleness. He kissed the valley between my breasts, his breaths making my skin wet.

He slowly moved back up, but the kissing stopped.

Now, he just stared at me, his brown eyes on mine, shifting back and forth slightly to take in the look on my face. His hand was still deep in my hair, but he didn't tug it aggressively. Seconds passed, but his intensity never waned. "I love you." The silence that followed those words was heavier than the words themselves. He said with such confidence and sincerity that it was obvious it wasn't something he blurted out in the heat of the moment. He'd felt this way for a while, and now he'd chosen to say it.

My hands stroked up his chest as my heart started to pound right against my rib cage, my pulse loud and vibrating, making my entire body shake. There was a moment of terror, as if those words were painful like a knife to the back. But then all those sensations passed because they weren't real. My previous life was behind me, all the numbness, all the fear. I was a new person now, my broken heart healed, my trust already placed in this man's hands. My eyes started to water as my hands moved to his neck, my arms hooking around and bringing him closer, our foreheads touching. "I love you too."

He closed his eyes before he released a quiet breath. His other hand tunneled into my hair, and he held himself on top of me, the special moment continuing even when the words were part of the past.

His mouth pressed a gentle kiss to mine before he raised his head back and looked into my face once more, a brand-new look in his eyes, like he was a brand-new man, complete because of the words I echoed back to him.

His thumb caught one tear as it dripped from the corner of my eye toward my ear. He smeared it away before his hand gripped my thigh and pinned it into place, his mouth moving over mine in a slow kiss.

He tilted his hips and guided himself inside, slowly, gently, deeply.

It was like our first time...because it was our first time.

We were different people.

Both vulnerable, both honest, both real.

My hands moved into his hair, and I kissed him as he made love to me, as he rocked me gently into the bed and took every piece of my heart for himself, to protect, to care for. Other women had been in this bed before me, but I knew I was the only one who mattered. I was the only one he'd taken like this, the only one he whispered those words to.

I hadn't thought I could ever feel this raw emotion, not after the way I'd been ripped apart. I'd been numb, unable to feel anything ever again. When you were broken like that, you never put yourself back together; you never felt anything so intense for another person.

But it happened...and it was stronger than before.

YOU MIGHT ALSO LIKE...

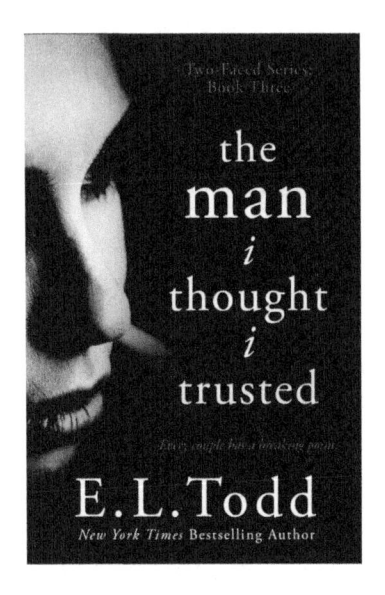

I'm not the kind of woman to hold a grudge, so I forgive Dax for the lies he told.

Now we're happy.

Happier than I ever thought I would be.

It's the first time we've ever really been together, completely honest with one another.

But maybe honesty isn't always the best policy...

Order Now

Printed in Great Britain
by Amazon